The Southern Cross

The
Southern Cross

STORIES

Skip Horack

A MARINER ORIGINAL · MARINER BOOKS
HOUGHTON MIFFLIN HARCOURT
BOSTON · NEW YORK
2009

For information about permission to reproduce
selections from this book, write to Permissions,
Houghton Mifflin Harcourt Publishing Company,
215 Park Avenue South, New York, New York 10003.

www.hmhbooks.com

Library of Congress Cataloging-in-Publication Data
Horack, Skip.
The Southern Cross : stories / by Skip Horack.
p. cm.
"A Mariner original."
ISBN 978-0-547-23278-2
1. Gulf Coast (U.S.)—Fiction. I. Title.
PS3608.072S68 2009
813'.6—dc22   2008053289

Book design by Melissa Lotfy

Printed in the United States of America

DOC 10 9 8 7 6 5 4 3 2 1

Many of these stories first appeared in the following publications: *Narrative* magazine (2008), *Epoch* (Fall 2008), the *Southern Review* (Winter 2008), *StoryQuarterly*
(Summer 2007), *Southern Gothic* (Spring 2007), *Louisiana Literature* (Winter 2007),
New Delta Review (Winter 2006), the *Southeast Review* (Winter 2006), *Sea Oats Review* (Fall 2005), and *Byline* (October 2005).

For my brother, Matt

The essence of dramatic tragedy is not unhappiness. It resides in the solemnity of the remorseless working of things.

—ALFRED NORTH WHITEHEAD
Science and the Modern World

Contents

Foreword

FOR THREE REASONS, I am very pleased to have played some small part in the fact of this fine book you hold in your hands. First, its author is my kind of writer, one who doesn't reserve his biggest and best for the larger canvas of the novel. This writer obviously reveres the short story as an art form in its own right. Every one of these stories serves up a unique world peopled by individuals who could, each of them, star in his or her own series. They are all epic-worthy. And yet, Skip Horack appears to have so much talent, talent to burn, that he can let each character occupy a single story, no more. That restraint—that simultaneous sense of abundance and tantalizing withholding—is primarily what made this collection stand out for me.

Second, the confidence in these stories' execution deeply impresses me. I appreciate the effect of reading them in concert with one another, how their shared presentation creates a world different from the one a single sustained narration like a novel might make, one that showcases moods and tempers and movements in the way the best music albums do, the way a roomful of a single painter's paintings allows the viewer fuller access to the act of creation, the breadth of the creator. What I mean to say is that the variety deepens the reader's intimacy with the writer's vision. I am awed by that vision, grateful for that gift.

Finally, I'll confess to swooning over people who make me laugh. My XM radio is tuned to the uncensored comedy channel; my favorite films include *Galaxy Quest* and *Groundhog Day*. I'm not embarrassed by this fact, exactly, but I feel I ought to offer it up as context when discussing the reasons I selected Skip Horack's *The Southern Cross* as this year's Bakeless Prize winner.

The competition was stiff. I had been assigning number ratings to the manuscripts and had to adjust from a scale of 1 to 5 to a scale of 1 to 10 because the submissions kept impressing me in ways that needed to be more subtly calibrated. The deciding factor came down to a single line in the middle of Horack's story "The Rapture." A pole dancer on her way home from work gets a lift from an evangelical male preacher. Upon dropping off the woman, the man asks in his raspy voice, "Sister, is there anything at all that you would like to pray for?"

And it was Horack's protagonist's delivery of this one-two punch line that cinched a KO victory: "I'll finish you off for fifty bucks. Amen."

ANTONYA NELSON

Spring

Caught Fox

I'M ROUNDING THE BEND at Johnson's Corner when I see Reverend Lyle has a girl waist deep in the concrete pool behind the church. He pauses the ritual and nods my way as I pass. His little brother Melrose was my split end back in the day, caught half the passes that set me up all-district. That still counts for something, so I lay off the gas to keep the dust down on the gravel road—away from the black women and their Easter hats. Maybe even give that shivering child's brand-new soul a shot at staying shiny and clean.

The hardwoods give way to farmland just past Laurel Baptist, and the Sawyers' pasture runs like a wide river alongside the Tunica Road. At the far end of the field, a fox pounces on mice under a blanket of low fog. I'm already late, but I pull the pickup over. It's nice to watch the fox, a burnt orange ghost dancing across misty green rye.

Jimmy's in the yard when I pull up, and, like I said, I'm late. Donna makes a show out of stomping her little ass around on the front porch, checking her watch like we both don't know it's broken. The ex can be mean as a snake so I stay in the truck and drink my coffee until she takes her act inside. I'm not looking for a fight on Easter morning.

It must be killing Donna that I get Jimmy today, one of maybe two Easters he's got left, absent a miracle. She likes Jimmy where she can keep a close eye on him, and, truth be told, he needs a mama like her. My skinny boy's retarded, no other way to put it.

Right now Jimmy's lying under the shade tree staring at his ant farm, just a gallon Mason jar I filled with black Mississippi dirt. He's like a mad scientist with those fire ants, and he lugs that heavy jar everywhere. He doesn't even notice me until I plop down next to him in the sycamore leaves and wish him a happy Easter.

"Daddy!" he says, the only person in the world ever truly happy to see Lucas Benton. We hug tight and I look over at the war he's started. Three carpenter ants, big and black, are fighting for their lives.

"Ant battle?"

Jimmy just nods, already back in his own world. Fire ants are swarming to the surface, and I watch his finger trace the side of the jar.

"I'm glad you like your farm," I say, pretty much to myself.

The jar was a present for Jimmy's tenth. I helped him leather-punch his initials into the lid for air holes, then together we searched the hay field behind my house, found the queen we needed laid up big and fat under a rotten fence post. You can't see her in the jar, but she's chambered somewhere deep in that honeycomb of tunnel, pulling her strings.

The carpenter ants are tougher than I'd have guessed, but they can't win. The fire ants run riot, will have their guests torn apart and butchered before long. When the show's over, I stand up and slap the broken leaves off the ass of my blue jeans.

"Wanna go look for a spider in the barn?"

"I got something better, Daddy."

Jimmy motions for me to hold on, then opens the lid of an old cigar box. The bottom is lined with fresh grass, and a mule killer, big as my thumb, swivels its head and tracks Jimmy with those spooky ghost eyes mantises have.

I settle back down on the heels of my boots as Jimmy drops this little gladiator into the jar. Fire ants versus a mule killer, now that's something worth seeing. I unbutton my shirt pocket and remove the can of Copenhagen I got tucked inside. Sure, the mantis is doomed—but in Jimmy's crazy pickle jar this might just be the closest thing yet to a fair fight.

Woodville's three sit-down restaurants are closed for Easter Sunday, so me and Jimmy drive on over to Centreville. All they got there is a chicken shack, but I figure we'll head to the hospital for our early lunch. I can't cook a lick, so I take quite a few of my meals at the cafeteria there. It's cheap, and, compared to what's served to the patients, the food's actually pretty damn good.

It's a meat-and-three setup, and today I tack greens, mashed potatoes, and fried okra onto the pot roast. Jimmy's not feeling hungry, or so he says. He's grumpy because I made him leave his jar in the truck. Still, Miss Effie's working the register, and she won't have none of that. She forces him to take a no-charge slice of cream pie. Women dote on my boy, I swear they do. I'd like to think he gets that from me. Donna would tell you different.

Church has let out and so the hospital's crowded with get-well visitors. I'm finishing up my lunch when Russell Sawyer ducks into the cafeteria. I stop by his table on the way to dump my tray.

"How you doing?" I dropped school back in '94 when Donna went pregnant, worked a few months at Russell's dairy farm before I got on at the creosote yard ten years ago. "Happy Easter," I say.

Russell looks up from the styrofoam cup cradled in his massive hands. "Oh, hey, Lucas. What you doing up in here?"

Jimmy doesn't know Russell all that well so he's sort of lagging back behind my right hip. He can be real shy around strangers, depending on his mood—and that can swing like a dog's tail. "Just getting something to eat." I pull Jimmy out from behind me like a magician, and he introduces himself like I taught him.

"Nice to meet you, son." Russell messes Jimmy's red hair and that makes them both smile. They'll be friends for life now. That's all it takes with Jimmy.

"How about you?" I ask. "Here for the coffee?"

Russell laughs. "Nah. We stopped by after church to visit Claudia's daddy."

"How's he doing?"

"He's doing." Russell unclips the thick tie he's wearing and opens the top collar of his dress shirt. Before he died, my old man had a brown suit just like the one Russell's got on. I wonder whether maybe it's the same one. Between the secondhand stores and the yard sales, clothes have a way of getting recycled in Wilkinson County.

"Saw a fox in your front field this morning."

"Yeah?"

"Sure did," I say, and that gives me an idea. "Okay if Jimmy and I lay down a trap? We're looking for something to do."

"Just mind where you put it, don't snap one of my pasture calves."

"You bet. Appreciate it."

We're saying our goodbyes when Amanda Sawyer walks through the door. She was close to Jimmy's age when she used to pester me in the dairy barn, but I reckon she's just about done with high school now. She's really turned into something

to look at, Amanda. Big brown eyes and shiny brown hair. I figure she'll be leaving this town soon. She'll ship out one day and
won't never look back.

"Thought I might find you hiding in here, Daddy." Amanda
leans over to kiss Russell on the cheek, and I shoot a sly glance
down the front of her church dress. "Mama's hunting you," she
says.

"You look pretty," says Jimmy. He takes his classes right next
to the high school, and Donna tells me that some of the older
girls look out for him.

"Why, thank you," says Amanda, laughing. Jimmy's latched
himself on to her leg, but she's real nice about it. She's got great
legs, cheerleader legs, all muscled up and curvy. When she hugs
me hello, my hand brushes across her hip, and the smooth slide
of fabric flat kills me. Nylons under a silk dress, that's a weak-
ness of mine. I got a few.

Now Russell's talking. "What year's that Chevy you drive?"
he asks. I step away from his baby girl and know straightaway
what he's getting at. We went over this maybe a hundred times
back when he was my boss.

"An '85, Mr. Russell."

"You be careful driving across my fields in that old truck,
we haven't had a good rain in a while."

"I'll stick to the roads, promise."

"And close all the gates? I don't want to be chasing cows on
Easter."

"I'll close them all behind me."

Amanda laughs. "You coming back to work for us, Lucas?"

"We're gonna trap a fox out in your field," Jimmy tells her.
It tickles me that he knows that. You can never tell what he'll
pick up.

"That so?" Amanda walks over to Russell and smoothes out

the polyester wrinkles on the back of his coat. "Then can Lucas give me a ride to the house, Daddy? I hate hospitals."

"Please let her come with us," Jimmy begs, then he whispers to Amanda, "I hate hospitals too." I can tell that makes everybody kind of sad, and that's the dark side of Jimmy sometimes understanding things better than we give him credit for.

Russell shrugs. "You mind, Lucas?"

Amanda answers for me. "Oh, he doesn't mind," she says. "He needs someone to remind him to close all those gates"—she tomboy-punches my shoulder—"not start any fires."

Jimmy claps his hands and Amanda passes him off to me so we can leave before Russell thinks of something else to worry about. I'm not sore about it though; her daddy's got a real good thing going on that farm. I'd worry too.

Dr. Cobb is a nice enough man, even looks a little like Santa Claus. But I'm not thrilled when he catches me in the parking lot out front of the ER. That's the tricky thing about eating at the hospital—getting away before a fucking doctor ruins my meal.

Amanda and Jimmy are already in the truck, and Dr. Cobb asks me how he's doing. The miss-a-beat spaces he puts between his words make it sound like he's speaking to a child, but that's just a doctor's way of asking if we've found anybody in the world willing to give a retarded boy a new heart. I grab a Budweiser out the ice chest in back of the truck and stare at him. That's my way of saying, We ain't, but thanks for fucking asking on my day off.

We don't get half a mile from the hospital before Amanda talks me into pulling over and giving her one of my beers, making a point of telling me that she's eighteen. Jimmy's always got to have the window so Amanda's squeezed in next to me, sipping, her dress gathered around her knees so I can work the stick. She lets me rest the side of my hand on her thigh when I'm between gears, and you know I'm not complaining.

The highway back into Woodville is plugged while everyone waits for a tanker to reverse into the Shell station. Cheerleaders are washing cars in the gas station's parking lot, and I watch a black girl shoe-polish CLASS OF '05 ROCKS DA HOUSE on the back windshield of a glistening Nissan Sentra.

"What's all that about?" I ask.

Amanda wipes her mouth. "We're raising money, figure people might be looking to give on Easter."

I shrug. I don't feel much like giving, Easter or ever.

Amanda whispers something in Jimmy's ear, and he ducks below the window at the same time as she reaches over and taps my horn. The cheerleaders look up from their charity and they don't see Jimmy giggling down by the floorboards with his ant farm. All they see is Amanda Sawyer sidled up next to Lucas Benton like she's a barrel racer on prom night. Amanda sends them a little wiggle wave with her bottle of Bud, and they step on their jaws as the traffic eases and we pull away.

Jimmy and Amanda play their game the whole way through town, and they can tell it's making me blush. Deputy Biggs, the one we call Needlenose, he damn near breaks his neck when he passes us in his cruiser. We see Donna's sister pulling into Treppendahl's, and I can't help but laugh. Truth be told, I'm really liking the idea of riding through Woodville with Jimmy out the picture, just Amanda by my side.

That's a hell of a thing for a daddy to be thinking. I curse myself as we pull off the blacktop and begin bucking across the washboard ruts that announce the beginning of the Tunica Road.

. . .

The twelve-pack's gone by the time I roll up on the Sawyers' big white farmhouse. We stretched the drive out as long as we could—stopped by my shed to gather trapping gear and took all the back roads—but the cheerleaders are expecting Amanda for the second shift. She needs to go on and change, head over to the car wash.

Amanda says she still has a few minutes and so she invites us inside for a cold drink. Jimmy lives off sweets, and he's out the truck before I can shut the engine down. I'm right behind him.

We get Jimmy situated with a bottle of cream soda and a pack of those Nabisco cookies that look like huge peanuts. Amanda heads upstairs to her room, leaves us sitting at the kitchen table. Jimmy's jar is resting between us on the Lucite, and we watch the fire ants work over the dried-out husk of the mule killer. My boy munches Nutter Butters while we wait to say our goodbyes.

Amanda told me I could have one of her daddy's High Lifes so I polish off a bottle, then ask Jimmy to sit tight while I hit the bathroom at the end of the hallway. A grandfather clock strikes two as I come out the john fumbling with my belt, and I bump right into Amanda standing there in her bikini.

She's wearing red gym shorts on the bottom, has the waist-band doubled over so they ride low. I step aside to let her pass but she puts her hands on my hips and sort of leans into me, makes me promise to stop by later and let her wash that dusty truck of mine.

"Of course," I say, "but only because it's for a good cause and all." And then Amanda Sawyer's standing on tiptoes in her flip-flops with her beer-cold tongue in my mouth. The midnight blue top of her swimsuit is pressed flat against my chest, and I feel a soft crush as it rubs back against her.

Jimmy's just around the corner, but we fool around pretty serious right there in the hallway. I'm a puppet master pulling at bikini strings when I hear Jimmy's chair chalk-scratch across the linoleum. I figure that means he's about to come looking, wants to show me something exciting happening in his jar. As much as it kills me, I have to pull back.

A thin thread of spit connects me to Amanda for a moment, then it snaps and falls back against my chin. Amanda giggles as she licks it away, and I think to myself that it's true what they say about the class of 2005. Those seniors really do rock the house.

I make my fox set on the no-cattle side of the barbed-wire fence, just before the Sawyers' pasture yields to thicket and pine. A scratch road cuts right through the middle of the field, and my truck's parked in the shade of a pecan tree maybe fifty yards away. Jimmy's napping on a horse blanket I laid down for him in the bed. He was tired from all his medications, and I figured he should catch some shuteye while I work. You don't want to get him too excited.

There's not much to a dirt-hole set. I dig a narrow tunnel about six inches deep, then drop in a couple of the frozen mice I sometimes use to pull the big catfish—the monster blues and flatheads—out of Lake Mary and the Mississippi.

My hole angles under a clump of ragweed, and a fox will have to step right onto the pan of a no. 2 coil spring to reach inside. That's the most important thing, tricking the fox into approaching from the right direction. And you have to do it in a natural sort of way. If the fox doesn't think he has a world of choices, he'll just pass on by.

Across the fence, a fat Holstein chews her cud and watches me finish off the set. I screen-sift black dirt over the trap, then splash the area with a bottle of fox urine to cover my scent. When I'm done I carry my gear on back to the truck, and the cow wanders away. Between thawed mice and fox piss, I smell like all hell. Jimmy's still asleep so I jump the fence again and take a deer trail down to the creek to wash off.

I linger awhile down by the water, just a series of pools connected by a thin trickle. It's a no-name creek to me, one more stream that feeds into the Buffalo. I sail a mulberry leaf from one pool to the next. A pod of whirligigs skitters past, and I scoop one up.

You hold a water bug to your nose, it smells a little like bubblegum. My hands still reek of fox piss so I smash the whirligig flat to make a soap of sorts. I begin working the broken body between my fingers, but I'm not sure it's helping. I catch a handful more and keep scrubbing away.

A car horn's blaring in the distance, but sound travels funny in a creek bottom. I don't realize it's blowing for me until the beep plays out steady for a good ten seconds. That's when I figure Jimmy's in some sort of bind. I hurry up the bank so fast I miss the deer trail, end up bushwhacking through greenbrier until I stumble back out into the clearing.

Donna's Datsun is parked over by the pasture gate, and the ex is leaned up against my truck, arm inside the open window, working the horn. I hop the fence and here she comes, all business. Donna's a forest fire coming across that field, and I shuffle over to meet her halfway. So maybe it wasn't such a good idea tooling around Woodville playing Jimmy-on-the-floorboard with Amanda Sawyer. It is a small town.

"What's going on?" I holler. She's wearing a church dress not all that different from Amanda's, and I wonder how much of her Easter she's spent driving around looking for us.

"Where's he at, you son of a bitch?" Donna gave Jimmy his

red hair, and right now hers is frizzed out and wild. I've done plenty to make her mad in my life, but when she rushes up on me, damn near shoves me to the ground, I can see from her wet green eyes that she's not so much mad as scared. And to tell the truth, that scares me.

"He's in the truck."

"No, he ain't."

That catches my attention. I brush past her and jog on over to the pecan tree and my pickup. She's right—no Jimmy, no jar—so I climb on top the cab for a better look.

The thin steel buckles under my weight as I scan the pasture, and I relax when I spot Jimmy way off on the far side of the field. I wave over to Donna but she only glares back, arms akimbo and looking like a gunslinger.

I call for Jimmy once or twice, but he's either too far away or he just ain't listening. Donna has finally decided to walk on over, so I climb down off the cab and crank the engine. Me and Donna in the Chevy, just like old times. I pull off the road and we start bouncing across the field like Russell Sawyer told me not to. "You see," I say. "He's fine. He just went looking around."

Now that Donna can see him she's calmed herself down. She wipes at her eyes and looks at me. "He's been with you all day?" she asks.

"Tell your sister to mind her own business." I see now that Jimmy has spotted us coming. He's standing next to his pickle jar and doing a little dance. "Yes," I tell her. "He was with us."

Donna laughs without smiling. "Us?"

"Me and Amanda."

"I know who you mean. What are you doing hanging around with a high-school girl?"

"Her daddy wanted me to give her a ride."

Again with that same laugh. "You're a goddamned fool, Lucas." She grabs me by my arm and the truck veers.

"Easy."

"Look me in the eye and tell me he was with you."

I'm not her husband no more so I won't do that. Instead I just tell her about the stupid game that Jimmy and Amanda were playing, leaving out second-base-in-the-hallway and a few other details. I know that Donna actually likes Amanda so I think she's all right with the story. But then again, I'm not so sure she's even listening anymore. She's staring straight ahead and looks, I don't know, tired.

I finish up and she sighs. "You still should have been watching him," she says.

That's not really something you can argue with, so I don't even bother trying to explain just how bad fox piss smells on a man's hands. I keep my mouth shut and drive on.

Things go south again when we catch up with Jimmy and realize that he's in pain and sobbing. I get out the truck and he keeps on dancing. He's covered in fire ants. Good Christ. I look down and see that he's kicked the top off an enormous ant pile. He's got dirt clear up to his elbows. "Son of a bitch," I say. "Get away from there."

Jimmy blows past me and runs to his mama. "Don't you curse him," says Donna, and then she strips him naked right there in the field. I pull the ice chest out the bed of my truck and she dunks his head inside, starts washing the ants from his thick hair. He's shivering from the cold water, and I can see red welts rising on his pale white skin. I fetch the horse blanket and we wrap him up tight. He's not happy but at least he's stopped crying.

"What were you doing, son?" I ask him.

At last Jimmy looks at me. "I wanted another queen," he says.

"What? Why?"

"Leave him alone," says Donna.

I rub the back of my neck until I settle. "It's okay," I say finally. "You'll be all right now." I tickle at his ribs. "We just need to get you some calamine."

Donna is smoothing out his hair, and her clean dress is dirty now. I forget myself, think this might be a good time to put my arm around her. Mistake. She slaps my hand away, shooting me a look that'd burn holes before she packs Jimmy into my truck. "Tell Daddy bye," she says.

Jimmy gives me a stiff-wristed wave but doesn't say anything that I can hear. Donna shuts the door behind him and he stares at me through the glass. I throw the ice chest in the bed as they pull off and leave me. I'm a scarecrow in that pasture watching Donna drive him on back to her car.

Visitation day's over, happy fucking Easter. I track down Jimmy's clothes but they're lousy with ants. I stuff them deep into a rabbit hole over by the fencerow, then go back and grab his pickle jar before I begin the long walk across the field. He'll want his ants later, so I'm cradling that jar like a baby. I'd hate to see those fragile tunnels collapse, they take so long to make.

I never do get my truck washed. Start to—even drive all the way back into town—but the football players have beaten me to the Shell station. They're in the middle of some kind of grab-ass water fight with the cheerleaders when I turn the corner. I see Amanda wrestling some hardleg for a hose and all of a sudden I feel like an asshole. She spots me but I creep on by. I'm watching her in the rearview. She goes on back to playing before I can shift to third gear.

Sundays are tough enough without it being Easter, and it's all downhill after that. I ain't got nobody to eat ham with, so I go looking for trouble.

And I find it soon enough. I pass Tommy Causwell on the highway and he flags me down. He's headed across the state line to find an open bar so I leave my truck at Dixie Creosote and hop on in.

We drink our way south to Baton Rouge, that chemical city. Across the river from the Cancer Alley refineries there's an all-night dive named the Firefly, then another called the Shift Change. We stay longer than's reasonable at both, and next thing I know it's four in the morning and I'm out front some fuck 'n' suck, waiting on Tommy to get his hand job so we can limp on home.

By the time Tommy drops me back off at the yard, it's almost dawn and I want to die. The turpentine stench of creosote bubbling away in the dip tanks flat gags me, and I puke up my empty stomach right there in the parking lot. Tommy pulls away laughing, covering me in a cloud of shell dust when he spins his tires. I'm doubled over sweating ice water, and all I want is to head back to the house, call in sick, and boil in the tub.

But a caught fox suffers, and a trapper should never put off checking his sets.

The stench of a possum fouls a good fox set forever, and that's just what I've got waiting for me in the pasture—a boar possum and a ruined fox set. He starts hissing like a loosed balloon when he spots me coming over the barbed-wire fence.

A filthy possum's not much use for anything. The pelt might fetch a buck or two, if you can find a buyer. But I figure Jimmy will get a kick out of the grizzled gray hide if I tan it up real nice, maybe tack it on his wall or something.

Dawn's breaking, and I'm cutting myself a green branch when I see an upstairs light flicker on in the Sawyers' distant farmhouse. I picture Amanda getting up for school, and the way I imagine it, her room's all sweet smells and yearbooks, teddy bears and pillow clouds.

I've got a .22 pistol in the truck, but there's a no-blood way to kill a possum. He's caught tight by the foreleg, so I start in with the sweet gum switch and work him over pretty good. He fights right on back for a while, but there's something in these fuckers that clicks when things go hopeless. I push too far and his eyes glaze over as he plays decoy dead. I drop the switch and put the steel toe of my boot right between his shoulder blades, wrapping the naked tail once around the meat of my hand. A quick tug and the spine snaps under my foot with a gravel crunch.

The sun's well up in the sky by the time I finish digging out my trap, and walking to the truck with my kill, I can't tell whether Amanda's light's still on or not. For a long while, I just sit behind the steering wheel staring at that farmhouse window. Spring fleas have left the possum for my hand and soon I get to scratching, Jimmy's forgotten pickle jar resting right there beside me.

Chores

EASY SYKES PULLED into his gravel driveway and parked alongside the singlewide trailer that he shared with his part-time father. Their two-acre lot was carved out of the front corner of a dairy farmer's hay field; a speckled Holstein had stretched her thick neck between strands of barbed wire and was feeding on Easy's lawn.

The grass was a foot tall in places. Easy looked across the highway and saw the pastor of Bethel Baptist pause from changing the message on his roadside church sign. The black man watched him, smiling big when Easy lifted a five-gallon gas can from the back of the Ford. Easy carried it across the yard, smiled himself when he saw the pastor place the final letters on that week's sentence sermon, telling the world: OUR CHURCH IS PRAYER CONDITIONED, PLEASE COME PRAY WITH US.

The riding lawn mower sat under a tarp lashed to a cluster of slash pines. Easy filled the tank, then began checking and replacing spark plugs. The sun was full up and steam rose from the yard as the morning dew burned away. By the time Easy was able to coax the ancient Deere to life, sweat had plastered his cotton shirt to his back, and the grass was dry enough to cut.

He worked the mower parallel to the highway, disengaging the blade as he passed over the damaged strip of yellow grass where his father liked to park his eighteen-wheeler. When he was home, the old man insisted that the trailer be kept cave cold and blacked out like his Peterbilt's sleeper, a familiar place to rest between runs where he could drink Coors oilcans and tell Easy stories about truck-stop romances, whiteout blizzards on Raton Pass. He never stayed long enough for his rig to actually kill the grass in the front yard, but the lawn sure did suffer for his visits.

Easy finished with the front and began cutting behind the trailer. A thick patch of ragweed grew along the back fence. Here, he busted a pair of quail that exploded across the hay field. They separated then disappeared into the pinewoods, and Easy tracked them, wincing as he imagined a clutch of eggs passing through the blade of his mower.

Later, the lawn finished, Easy drank his father's beer on the back deck and watched the hen quail scratch along the fence-row for the remains of her nest. From a distant brush pile the male whistled *bobwhite* twice, then fell silent when a mockingbird took up the call.

The Journeyman

THE MORNING BEFORE he left for South America, a black girl in beaded braids came calling on Clayton. She was nine, maybe ten, and she introduced herself as Kenyatta before explaining that—with the help of her Bible—she had killed the serpent living under his house. Clayton had been expecting his wife when he heard the knock at the door, figured Jolie had forgotten her keys at the diner again. Shirtless in faded 501s, he stepped into a pair of Red Wings and joined Kenyatta on the porch, lighting a cigarette while he considered girl-in-a-church-dress and serpent-under-the-house.

From the crumbled corner of Press and Dauphine, a timid cavalry of neighborhood boys looked on, legs cocked on the pedals of their battered bikes. Clayton followed Kenyatta onto the sidewalk, and the oft-chased children flushed like plantation quail, scattering deep into the Marigny. Kenyatta ignored their retreat, but bold as she was, Clayton saw that she was careful to avoid the cracks in the concrete.

Kenyatta led him onto the vacant lot that ran alongside his clapboard shotgun, then began picking her way through the shattered glass and ragweed. At the far end of the torn half acre, she showed him where she had cornered the snake against the rusted-out shell of a Kenmore icebox. A few feet away, the two halves of a Bible—the binding cleft somewhere near the Testament divide—lay next to a fat water moccasin writhing in death spasms. Ocean tides of muscle relaxed and contracted under pecan brown scales.

"I've been watching that serpent," said Kenyatta. "Every time I try to kill him he slides back up under your house." She smiled. "But I caught him sleeping today." Clayton listened as Kenyatta told him how after crippling the moccasin with chunks of asphalt, she had launched her church Bible at the poor creature and, in a miracle of sorts, opened the snake's head with the hard edge of the Holy Book.

Clayton explained to her that the moccasin was very poisonous, very dangerous, that Kenyatta should stay away from all snakes, that she was better off keeping to the sidewalks.

Kenyatta just shrugged.

The mystery, the part Clayton couldn't figure, was how a cottonmouth ever came to live under a house in New Orleans. The Mississippi was staged spring high, and perhaps the snake had been forced from the weed bank by the rising river. Perhaps, even from the other side of the levee, the moccasin had been drawn to calmer waters in the Marigny, to that cool collection of rain that had softened the foundation of Clayton's home and sent cracks racing up the plaster walls of the shotgun.

Kenyatta claimed her grandmother would whip her if she came home without her King James. She demanded that Clayton buy her a new one. Too tired to argue with the logic of a child, he offered up a crumpled ten and she left him alone with the dying snake and the broken Bible.

Clayton ground the snake's head into the dirt with the toe of his boot, then watched a rundown Volvo turn the corner on Press Street. It stopped in front of his house just long enough for Jolie to step out. She was wearing her work uniform, and handicapped by knockoff French Market Chanels, she never saw him as she walked up their porch steps and into the house.

A breeze washed over the lot, and a page from the Bible—thin as cigarette paper and flecked with snake blood—broke free from cheap glue and pinned itself against Clayton's leg. Kneeling, he read the first full passage he came to. A story about ancestry, about ancients begetting ancients. Irrelevant Scripture about people who lived for centuries, back when such a thing was possible. He shifted his leg and watched the page blow away.

Clayton stepped into the kitchen. "Hey there, Mrs. Godeaux."

Jolie raised her hand for silence as she finished counting the wrinkled cash piled in front of her. She divided her tips into smooth, even stacks of ones and fives that she folded and placed in her purse. "Where you been?" she asked him as she took the pins out of her dirty blond hair and shook it loose.

Clayton wasn't up for explaining why he'd had to give a little girl money to buy a Bible. His wife rose from the table and he grabbed her wrist, pulled her close. Exhausted, she buried her head in his chest as he kneaded the tense muscles at the base of her neck. He felt her relax as she leaned against him and dug her hands into the front pockets of his jeans.

"So Mr. Quinn called this morning," he said.

Jolie lifted her head to look into his eyes.

"A spot opened on a ship leaving for Argentina tomorrow."

"Tomorrow?"

"Last-second deal. He knows a captain who needs to replace a deck hand laid up in Charity."

"How long?"

"Three months." Clayton scratched the side of his neck and shrugged. "Four months tops, depending on weather."

Jolie winced. "That's all you need, right? Three more months?"

"Yeah." He stroked her hair with the back of his hand. "I just hoped I'd get a longer break between trips."

"You took it already?"

"Might be months before he can find me another berth."

"That a yes?"

"Yeah. I'm sorry."

"No, we knew this might happen. But we need to do something today."

"You're tired, sugar. We'll do something tonight before you go in."

"You sure?"

Clayton soft-kissed her full on the lips and saw the half circles ashed on the smooth Cajun skin beneath her glass blue Catahoula eyes. "Positive," he said. "Get some sleep."

Jolie took his hand and pulled him toward the white-noise hum of the window unit in the back of the house. Reaching their bedroom, she spun like a dancer and fell backward onto the mattress. Clayton sat down beside her and, like he did every morning when she came home from work, placed her legs across his lap. One at a time, he untied her tennis shoes and slipped them off her feet.

"Tell me about Africa," she whispered.

So Clayton lit a cigarette and told her about the ports in Africa. About Liberian stowaways and revolution. Open-air markets where honest-to-God warriors sold Zippos and antelope no bigger than dogs. Then, leaving talk of Africa, he massaged her feet and told her about the beautiful fabric that he would bring back from South America. The whales he would see in the shipping lanes on his way home.

• • •

They had been high-school lovers—the option quarterback and the queen of the Duck Festival—and then one day it was 2004, and they were twenty-one apiece and both still living at home. That summer they spent Independence Day in a cinder-block roadhouse on the edge of the Cajun prairie, watching the Banded Mallards warm up as their relationship cooled off. They were beer-chasing tequila when Jolie cried and told him that she couldn't do this anymore. She needed out of the rice fields of Gueydan and places like the Blue Goose Lounge. Desperate, gasping for air, Clayton brought her out to the starlit parking lot and told her that he was through with all the drinking and the drugs and the being shiftless. He promised her New Orleans. Falling to his knees onto crushed oyster shells, he begged her to marry him.

Within a month, they were renting the one-bedroom shotgun in the Marigny. Jolie found work waitressing in the Quarter, and a black man named Quinn Freeman hired Clayton to stevedore the Press Street Wharf. "You'll be working with some tough sons a bitches," Quinn had warned him. "Just mind your own business and you'll be all right."

Quinn's crew arrived at dawn and worked ten-hour shifts in the September heat. They were all thick black men, prison-inked and scarred. Clayton watched them stumble off the city bus in the morning and imagined their nights were harder than anything Quinn threw their way. He stayed clear.

The best jobs—operating the power winch and crane, the lift truck and grain trimmer—those went to the men who had been around the longest. As a rookie, Clayton worked pure labor on the dock with a man named Redfish less than four months out the farm at Angola. Without sharing a word, Clayton and Redfish would lash and shore cargo, attach slings and hooks to crates and containers, reposition the spouts of the trimmer after a hatch filled with grain. When they broke at noon, the others threw dice against the side of the warehouse, and Clayton would sit alone atop a granite boulder on the bank of the Mississippi and eat the sandwich Jolie had made for him. It was a living.

But during his second week working, too impatient to wait for the dock to clear, Clayton pulled a pallet out from under a suspended container, moving away moments before the sling slipped and a thousand pounds of steel came crashing down. He was trembling even before Redfish grabbed him by the back of the neck and slammed him against the side of a forklift—told him that he was a stupid white boy, that no job was worth dying for.

Clayton began to have nightmares, dreams in which he didn't step out from under the shipping container in time. He would watch himself being crushed and wake up in a cold sweat, punish Jolie as he flailed around searching for more of her warm body.

The thing Clayton could not understand was why, with all of his bad history, that reckless dash under a suspended container to move a worthless pine pallet was the one act that he could not forgive himself for. At work, over the roar of commerce and cursing men, he would hear the voice of his bedridden father, hand mangled by a rice husker, telling him over and again that heavy machinery and flexible people simply did not mix.

Though never a coward, Clayton became convinced he would be killed on the job. These thoughts paralyzed him at work, and a week after the accident, haunted by this bizarre demon, he went to see Quinn and asked if there was anything else available, maybe something on one of the tugboats.

Quinn was sitting behind the desk in his cluttered office scratching at his graying beard. He looked up from the racing form he was studying. "The insurance folks won't let me hire anyone onto a tug unless they have their Z-card and at least six months' sea time." He blew a cloud of cigarette smoke at the ceiling. "So the answer's no, I don't have nothing else available." Quinn returned to his racing form and Clayton came closer. He watched the cords of muscle in the man's forearm flex as he circled the sixth horse in the seventh race with a grease pencil.

"So then how do I do it?" Clayton asked, refusing to leave.

"Do what?"

"Get the license? The sea time?"

Clayton bought a new pair of coveralls at the Wal-Mart on Tchoupitoulas before driving out to the lakefront to find Quinn. He parked the truck and spotted him drinking coffee at his usual Sunday-morning spot, a line of fishing rods staked out along the seawall in front of him.

"Hey, hey."

"All right, Cajun. What you know good?"

"Catching anything?"

Quinn nodded at the five-gallon bucket resting a few feet from his lawn chair, and Clayton walked over to look inside. When his shadow passed over them, two monster blue crabs blew bubbles of angry sea foam and lifted their thick claws in defense.

"Pretty crabs," said Clayton. "They look fat."

"Just lagniappe. They're yours if you want them."

Clayton considered the offer as he dug a soft pack of Camels from the front pocket of his yellow guayabera, a sun-bleached gift from a Latin shipmate. He tapped out two cigarettes and offered one to Quinn.

Quinn waved him away. "I got my menthols."

"Don't know how y'all smoke those things." Clayton smiled. "Taste like fiberglass."

"Y'all as in 'you people'?"

"Exactly."

Quinn shook his head. "I'd be careful. You're darker than a Schwegmann's bag yourself."

Clayton laughed and knelt down next to him. Out in the lake, a raft of white pelicans was pushing its way toward the shoreline.

"Shouldn't you be packing or something?" Quinn asked. "Spending time with your pretty wife instead of out here baiting me?"

"I'm leaving, I'm leaving. I just wanted to come out here and say thanks."

"Bullshit. You wanna make sure I'll keep my word before you hop on a ship for another three months."

"That too."

"Like I told you already, you finish up your sea time and I'll make you a deck hand. Spend a year as a deck hand, pass the exam, I'll make you an apprentice. After that, hit all your marks and don't piss me off, I'll make you a captain."

Clayton stared out at Lake Pontchartrain. The morning haze had lifted off the water, and in the bluebird distance he could see the faint outline of the causeway bridge to the North Shore. "Why bother giving me this shot?" he asked.

Quinn looked over at him. "I'm not doing you any favors, kid. Trust me, make captain under me, you'll have earned it."

"But that ain't no answer."

Quinn sighed. "Fine," he said. "You know anything about horseracing?"

"Some. Me and Jolie used to hit the races over in Lafayette."

"Well, I know a whole hell of a lot about horseracing."

Clayton nodded, agreeing that was so.

"Know what my tiebreaker is?"

"What you mean?"

"When I have two horses I can't decide on. You know how I go and break the tie?"

"Tell me," said Clayton.

"The jockeys. Horses come and go, but if you get a feel for the jockeys, you'll do okay. Good jockeys usually ride good horses. Crap jockeys usually ride crap horses."

"Except when they don't."

"I said usually. Ain't nothing in life always. Give me fifty-one percent and I'm happy."

"Makes sense."

"Of course it makes sense, and that's how I run my business. A Thoroughbred is only as good as its jockey. A tugboat is only as good as its captain." Quinn refilled his coffee mug from a silver thermos. "Look, before you I bluffed off at least a dozen guys with the same deal. Not one of them was willing to get on a ship for six months. So I guess that says something about you."

Clayton smiled. "I knew if I stayed out here long enough I could get you to say something nice about me." Quinn grunted and Clayton laughed. The pelicans were feeding on a school of mullet a hundred yards down the seawall. "Go cast around those birds, boss. There might be a big red cruising for scraps."

"Goddamn it, don't tell me how to fish." But Quinn rose from his chair and grabbed a spare rod rigged with a gold spoon. He shook Clayton's hand. "Be careful out there, son. I'll see you in three months."

Clayton watched Quinn jog down the seawall, then he walked to his truck to find something to put the two crabs in.

That afternoon, Clayton boiled an inch of water in a stockpot and began steaming the blues. Jolie would be hungry in a few hours, and he planned to surprise her with breakfast in bed.

Crabmeat omelets like the ones they had eaten during their honeymoon on Mobile Bay.

He was in good spirits because he enjoyed cooking and because, driving home from the lakefront, he had experienced a vision. Clayton was stopped at an Elysian Fields red light when a stray Mardi Gras bead—suspended on a telephone line for decades, perhaps—somehow broke free in the breeze and landed square on the hood of his pickup. An Asian woman shuffling across the intersection hesitated when she spotted the strand of plastic pearls, a relic from when parades still rolled in that part of town. Clayton gestured for her to pick them up, and, smiling, she lifted the beads from the hood of the Ford, then stepped back onto the sidewalk just as the light switched to green.

But that wasn't the vision, that was real.

The vision came because the wonderful old lady had been wearing a beautiful silk kimono and—like whenever he saw something beautiful—Clayton had thought of Jolie. Driving home, he pictured his wife in a kimono and, doing so, began to imagine that she was no longer a waitress serving drunks in an all-night diner. Instead, she was a hostess at some young, hip restaurant off Magazine or Prytania. A place really more like a bistro. Clayton saw her checking reservations and wearing the silk kimono, her blond hair pulled back and pierced with a pencil. He would come in after a day on the water, and, no matter how busy she was, she would find him a table, a good table, a table in the bar where he could watch her work while he ate his dinner. And the people she worked with—young college kids and artists, for the most part—they would tease them both about their clipped Vermilion Parish accents. But the girls would also copy Jolie's walk and try to mimic her toughness. And the men, the bartenders and the kitchen crew, they would call Clayton Captain and spend their smoke breaks at his table, pumping him for stories about the river and his time at sea. Finally Jolie would seat the last customers and be let go for the night. They'd drive to the sweet little home they had bought in the Bywater, and Clayton would be the only man ever lucky enough to slide the kimono's cool sleekness off her warm body.

Clayton sat at the kitchen table picking clean his two crabs and smiled because he knew that now it was this vision, Jolie as a savvy-shining-hostess, that would sustain him at sea. The vision that—even on the slippery, windswept deck of a flag-of-convenience freighter—would come to replace his crushed-by-a-shipping-container nightmare.

The crabmeat was cooling in the fridge, and Clayton was sprawled out under the Ford. A thin sheet of cardboard protected his bare back from the street as he contemplated the pair of small, white-stockinged legs that had appeared alongside his truck.

"That you, Kenyatta?"

"Yeah, it's me," she said. "You broke down?"

"Just changing the oil, baby." He didn't want the old pickup giving Jolie any problems while he was away.

"I come by to warn you."

"Yeah?" Clayton slid the socket onto the drain plug, grunting as he gave the wrench a hard twist. "About what?"

"God and Jesus are up to something."

"That so?"

"Reverend Gray says they gonna punish this city soon enough."

A car alarm started up just a few blocks over, and Clayton grinned to himself. "Yeah," he said. "I imagine they will."

He spun the wrench as Kenyatta spoke of discipline coming from above, how God would not abide the vice and corruption that had washed ashore on that big bend in the river. "Bad dealings are afoot." She stomped a buckled shoe, pretty and polished, hard on the pavement. "You need to be careful."

"I will," Clayton promised. "Thanks for thinking of me."

"You already had a serpent show up under your house," Kenyatta reminded him.

"That's true. I surely did." He finished unthreading the plug with his fingers, and a rush of spent oil, still warm from his drive out to the lakefront, spilled down into the catch pan. He brushed away the flecks of rust and dirt that had settled onto his face. "You're a voodoo child, for sure. You know that?"

But Kenyatta didn't answer. Clayton glanced over and saw that she had left him alone.

Spooky as she was, he was a little sorry to see her gone. It was sort of nice having her around, his steady lookout for pestilence and plague—a friend to help him recognize the angels among us and signs from God. She was right, in a way, they really were everywhere.

The Gulf Sturgeon Project

L ANDON DRAINED THE LAST swallow of bourbon from the plastic coffee mug he'd found in his motel room. A dark-haired woman was throwing a cast net from the fuel dock beneath his window. She released the net lasso-even and heavy onto a bubbling school of mullet while, downriver, noisy gulls chased a trawler under the Highway 98 bridge and back to Apalachicola. Onboard, young men in filthy white boots broke from sorting shrimp on the afterdeck. They waved to the woman, and she smiled big to the boys as she arranged herself for another throw.

With a little effort, Landon could imagine Gulf sturgeon swimming somewhere beneath that beaten trawler. His Gulf sturgeon. The five spawning females Cassie had helped him affix satellite pop-up tags to the previous spring. They were massive fish. Six, seven, even eight feet long. The largest of his research subjects—the one Cassie had dubbed Bertha—weighed over two hundred pounds and was pushing thirty years old.

The tags were programmed to release at midnight. They would bob to the surface of the river, and, thousands of miles above, the Argos satellite system would locate those tiny computers and begin downloading all the data they had collected over the past year. Finally Landon would have the mountain of data he needed to prepare his dissertation. He wondered if Cassie even remembered that they were supposed to be here tonight, that they were supposed to share this moment together. He pulled the cell phone from the back pocket of his shorts again. Maybe she would call. Maybe she would still come.

Landon returned to watching the sunset shrimp boat diesel upriver, the men working hard but no doubt already making plans to meet up later with their girls at some riverfront bar, a place where they would pay cash for salty steamed oysters and pitcher after pitcher of cold draft beer. In high school, Landon had spent his summers fishing crabs on Mobile Bay. He watched those men and suddenly he was certain that he would have been happier as a commercial fisherman. A life without research or dissertations. A life of just being out there on the water.

If Landon was Highway 98, Cassie was A1A. A South Florida beach girl who collected seashells in the Keys as a child and later, as a teenager, rode nesting loggerheads into the rising tide until the ancient turtles left her treading water in the midnight Atlantic. Or so she said.

They had been paired together as instructors of a freshman biology lab during their first semester as grad students at Florida State. She was loose-limbed and tan, with a husky voice that made him think of women in old movies. A week into fall classes, they were helping a hung-over Theta dissect a bonnet shark when Landon felt Cassie's weight shift against him. It was a simple thing really, just denim brushing denim and her hip pressed against his thigh. But Landon didn't pull away, and after that, well, it was just a matter of time.

And that time did come. Less than a month later he bumped into her in the parking lot of Po' Boys. He was leaving for Panama City. The pompano were migrating and he planned on night-fishing the surf. She wished him luck and then went on inside. He was pulling onto Pensacola Street when she came running up to his window. "So," she said, "would you mind so much if I tagged along?"

Of course he wouldn't. Not one bit.

They hit the interstate just after dark. Cassie perched her brown legs on the dusty dashboard of his old Bronco and leaned close to spin the radio dial. For laughs, she settled on the local AM broadcast of a high-school football game, then, fifty miles down I-10, Landon broke for gas next to an outlet mall that sold nurse uniforms and towels by the pound. He was filling the tank when she walked out of the station with a six-pack of Budweiser tall boys. Back on the road, the football game tied, Cassie offered him a beer and bet him twenty bucks that Port St. Joe would beat Carrabelle in the second half.

They were just outside of Panama City when Port St. Joe sealed the win with a two-point conversion. Landon dug two tens from his pocket but Cassie pushed the money away, would only accept the cash if he agreed to let her buy him a drink. Landon nodded and Cassie smiled as she slid her cigarette through a crack in the window. In his rearview mirror, he saw the Marlboro hit the asphalt and explode, bounce, and explode again before disappearing altogether.

He pulled off at a locals' bar on the north side, the pine-tree-and-boiled-peanuts side, of 98. The place was crowded with miniature-golf pros and charter-boat captains, airbrush artists and lifeguards. Cassie brought the house down singing kara-oke "Bobby McGee," and the bouncer gave her a plastic orchid so that later—after she had talked Landon out of fishing and they'd crossed the highway to walk the beach—she was wear-ing that fake flower in her chocolate hair when they made love in the dunes on a blanket of broken sea oats.

They finished up and lay there together in the sand for a long while. Cassie whispered stories in his ear while he smoked her cigarettes and watched ghost crabs wage their moonlight campaigns. "Have you ever come close to drowning?" she asked him.

Landon thought on it. "Not really," he said. "I was caught in a rip tide once but I got out okay."

"Everybody has rip-tide stories."

"I guess."

"When I was little, one pulled me from the shallow water right off Miami Beach."

"Yeah? How old were you?"

"Seven, I think."

"Jesus. What happened?"

"That's the funny thing," said Cassie. "Even as I was watching everyone on the beach panic and fade away I knew to just relax and ride the current."

Landon leaned over and kissed her forehead. "Smart girl," he said.

"But my father almost died swimming after me."

"I bet."

"We met up on the beach after it finally spit us both out." Cassie sat up in the sand. "Want to know what I asked him?"

"Tell me."

Cassie let her voice rise into that of a little girl. "Daddy, can I do it again?" She laughed and the woman was back. "Can you imagine?"

Later, Landon would remember that story and realize that she had been breaking up with him from the beginning.

A waitress was wiping down tables when Landon shuffled into the restaurant and apologized for being the late customer on a slow night. He offered to leave but the pretty girl just slapped him sweetly with her towel, then flipped the sign on the door. "Nice shirt," she said.

He was wearing the red Hawaiian that Cassie had bought for him. "Thanks," he said.

"Makes you look like Jimmy Buffett."

"All right."

She laughed. "Have a seat wherever. My name's Sunny."

Landon settled onto a stool at the empty bar and hoped that might make things easier on her. He asked for a beer and she poured him a draft with a grace that he recognized along with her cutoff khakis and T-shirt. She had dark eyes and dark skin and dark hair. "I think I saw you earlier," he said, "with a cast net on the dock."

"You staying next door?"

"Yeah."

Sunny handed him a plastic menu with sharp edges. "Then I think I saw you watching me from your window."

"Not just you."

"Fine. Not just me."

"You're good with a cast net. I can appreciate that."

"Oh yeah? Where you from?"

"Alabama. Fairhope."

"Roll Tide."

"You're from 'Bama?"

"You know Atmore?"

"Yeah, I know Atmore."

"I grew up on the Poarch Creek Indian Reservation. Daughter of the chief himself."

"No kidding?"

"I wouldn't lie."

Landon watched her head off and was glad she was working because she was young and pretty and cheerful, and that helped take the edge off being semi-drunk and alone in a quiet restaurant. When she returned he ordered the special and after a short while she brought him a plate loaded with fried mullet and coleslaw and cheese grits. She placed his dinner on the bar, and he stopped her as she turned to leave again. He was eager to talk all of a sudden. "How'd you wind up here?" he asked.

"I got married to a Marine." Sunny refilled Landon's beer from the line of taps behind the bar. "I'm living with his parents until he comes back from Afghanistan."

Sunny rapped at the bar with her knuckles, and Landon glanced at the thin gold band on her hand. He wasn't a kid anymore. At this point in his life he should be noticing these things. "How long's he been over there?" he asked.

"Close to a year now."

"That's gotta be tough." What a perfect thing to say. Landon shut up and finished his meal while she washed glasses at the sink behind the bar. On the television in the corner, the Braves were playing the Padres out on the West Coast and putting it to them. He sipped on his beer and watched the ballpark crowd dwindle.

Sunny finished with the glasses and fixed herself a vodka rocks. She sat down across from him at the bar and rubbed her neck with her left hand as she drank with her right. "So how about you?" she asked. "What brings you to Apalach?"

"Gulf sturgeon."

"Fish?"

He nodded and told her all about the Gulf sturgeon project, how at midnight the coordinates of the released tags would be forwarded to his cell phone. For the first time in a year, he would know whether his sturgeon had returned to the Apalachicola to spawn. Whether his fish were even still alive. Whether the project had been worth all the trouble.

Sunny frowned at him. "So for the past year you've been waiting around for this day?"

"Pretty much. The satellite can't locate or read the tags while they are underwater." Landon shrugged. "I'm here on faith."

"In what? Technology or sturgeon?"

"Both, I guess."

"Tell me something."

"Yeah?"

"Couldn't you have just stayed in Tallahassee?"

Landon tore a wet corner off the napkin pinned beneath his sweating glass. "I had sort of planned to meet someone here," he said. "We were supposed to celebrate the end of the project—or at least this part of it."

"A girl?"

Landon allowed a thin smile.

"I take it she's not in the Marines."

"Not quite. But you never know with her."

"She coming?"

"No."

Sunny raised her drink and their glasses clicked together.

The Braves did win. They won big, in fact, and after the game, a white-toothed man opened the late news with a story from Iraq. The talking head went heart-attack serious as the camera cut to a grainy video of a reporter begging for his life. Landon saw Sunny look away and so he grabbed for the remote control resting on the bar.

He killed the television, and Sunny thanked him softly. She trembled as she poured herself another vodka, then caught him watching her for the second time that day. She walked out from behind the bar. "Come on," she said. "There's something I want to show you."

"What?"

"A surprise." She took his hand and pulled him toward the door.

The restaurant opened out onto the water. Landon followed her to the edge of the fuel dock, and they watched in silence as the moon rose clean and bright over the Apalachicola. After the moonrise Sunny retrieved a cardboard flat of crab bait from the dock cooler, then began tossing frozen scraps of menhaden into the river. Landon was confused until he saw a collection of tarpon appear in the marina, rising and falling as they sucked down the oily fish in great gasps. Sunny worked the tarpon closer, and the largest of them surfaced alongside the dock to take a frozen pogy directly from her hand. Sunny laughed like a child, and for a moment—looking at her backlit by the full moon, reflected by the silver flash of a rolling tarpon—Landon could not imagine her as anything but the Poarch Creek princess she had claimed to be.

The marina's tarpon fed, Landon walked Sunny across the clamshell parking lot to her truck. She leaned against the side of an old blue Dodge and glanced at her watch. "Less than two hours until midnight, you know."

Landon nodded.

"Stop by the next time you pass through Apalach," she said. "Let me know how your project turned out."

"I will. I promise." Landon opened the door of the pickup for her, but she just smiled and watched him for a moment. Long enough that he could no longer meet her gaze, and so he stared instead at his flip-flop, drawing chalk circles in the shell dust.

"You're going to be okay," she said. "Both of us are."

"Yeah, I know." He looked up at her. "We've still got our fish, right?"

Sunny laughed and leaned in close to him until her hands were flat against his chest. She kissed him on the cheek before sliding into the cab of her truck. The door closed shut behind her, and Landon backed away as the diesel shuddered and then started. The pickup was pulling off when Sunny stopped and rolled down her window. "In another lifetime?"

Landon smiled. It was something Lauren Bacall would say, something Cassie would say in her own husky rhythms. He called back to Sunny. "Yeah," he said. "In another lifetime." But he didn't say it in any bitter sort of way. Watching her drive off, he knew that she was exactly what he'd needed on that night in that lifetime.

A map of the Panhandle coastline was spread out across the table, and Landon confirmed that four of his tags had surfaced in the Apalachicola—two just beneath the big dam near the Florida-Georgia line, another two within a few miles of where he was now sitting.

But the fifth tag confounded him. That fifth tag contradicted everything he knew about predicting the tendencies of Gulf sturgeon. Those last coordinates fell far off the chart. Landon consulted another map and realized that Bertha had strayed three hundred miles west of her home stream. In fact, as of midnight, she was just north of New Orleans and traveling up the Mississippi River.

A week later, on the last day of spring, Landon took his john-boat north of Tallahassee and fished a far, empty corner of Lake Jackson. Push-poling through the water hyacinth at dusk, he bumped a pair of wood ducks that flew off squealing to roost in a distant cypress swamp. They were local birds—ducks somehow born without the instinct to migrate north—but in a few months the teal would return to join them in the lake, and soon the widgeon and other big ducks would follow.

A ridge of hardwoods ran along the north shore of the lake, solid save for a wide fairway of lawn that plunged like a scar from the foot of an eggshell mansion on the hilltop. Black men in white jackets floated through a linen crowd scattered across the great lawn. A slight shift in the evening breeze carried piano music across the water, and to Landon it sounded like glass breaking gently.

He worked his boat closer to the party as he cast his spinner bait. Tucked among cypress knees was a boathouse where he and Cassie had once trespassed and made love. She was a fool for that kind of thing. He supposed they both were.

Landon thought back to the late-night phone message Cassie had left while he slept in the Apalachicola motel. It had been a bar-parking-lot sort of call, and she sounded a little drunk as she asked how the project had turned out. There were a lot of things Landon wanted to tell her, entire conversations he had practiced after dissecting her message—but in the end he just left it alone, never returned the call.

And so he never told her how the depth and temperature data showed that Bertha had left her home stream too soon. That she was forced into the deeper waters of the Gulf when Tropical Storm Bonnie blew across Apalachicola Bay in August. That at least one of the five journeys had been an anomaly, the wanderings of a lost and confused creature. No, he would never share this with Cassie. Landon kept all that to himself because finally he decided that the Gulf sturgeon project really didn't have anything to do with her. It was, after all, his dissertation.

Summer

Junebelle

I SIT STARING out the window, waiting for Patience. "We have a lake, ma'am," she said on the first day we met. "Did you ever go fishing when you lived in New Orleans?" Now there was a king question. I most certainly did not. That's exactly what I told the silly girl.

I've been living in this so-called retirement community for a full week now, and I still can't believe Patience ever asked me such a thing. It was almost worth the humiliation just to see Selby and Edward wince—although it's something that they were probably laughing about as soon as they drove back out through the sliding electric gate that seals us in here at Witness Oaks. My daughter is a funny one. "Lord," she would say, "can you imagine Mother sitting in this July sun with a cane pole?" And then the two of them would head over to Baton Rouge Country Club in that shiny black tank of theirs. Selby would read a paperback by the pool while Edward played golf. Golf. My Jack never played a day in his life. I didn't know how good I had it.

This lake they have here, by the way, is a pond. I can see it from the tiny sunroom of my apartment. It's pretty enough—what with the lily pads and the cattails—but if it's a lake, then I'm a Vanderbilt. Between meals I now spend my days gawking at that hot brown puddle from the armchair in my sunroom. The shallow-water edges get steady visits from herons and egrets, and the evening music of the frogs almost drowns out the cars passing along the other side of the red-brick fence that surrounds this place. So that's nice. I'll admit that—but the turtles seem to be at plague level, and just this morning I counted close to thirty of their little black heads. I mention this to young Patience when she finally comes to check my blood pressure. Her uniform is so white against her dark skin that it hurts my eyes.

"That's a lot of turtles, Miss June."

"Too many," I say. "They'll eat all your fish up."

Patience puts the cuff around my arm and smiles to herself when I say that. That makes me think that all the staff here have been talking, that there's been some sort of memo passed around instructing them not to ask Miss June anything about fish or fishing. You can say whatever to the people working here and they'll just grin back at you like children. As she's a colored girl, Patience has never seen the inside of Baton Rouge Country Club, I'm sure—but it's not really all that difficult for me to picture her there, sitting beside the pool with my pretty daughter and laughing, filling Selby in on everything that her pistol of a mother did that day. Spies, I see all of them as spies.

"Turtles eat fish?" asks Patience.

Her hair is shaved close to her head like a soldier's, and I'm studying on the perfect smoothness of her skull. "Never mind," I tell her.

"You know they're having a picnic tomorrow?"

"Of course I do."

"So you going then?"

"That's what they tell me."

Patience nods and then pins the stethoscope in her ears. I close my eyes and wait for her to finish pumping on that black bulb. The cuff tightens and that hurts a little. I guess Patience sees me flinching because she starts rubbing gently on my shoulder. "We almost done," she says. Finally I hear Velcro tearing and she rips the thing off. "Wonderful," says Patience. "You doing real good, Miss June. Real good."

My apartment has two doors: one that leads outside to the fishing grounds and another that opens up into a wide and carpeted hallway. I didn't realize how many of us were living here until I first walked down that hall. Door after door after door. And that's just the South Commons. They've got three other big buildings, not to mention some standalone homes and townhouses sprinkled here and there through the live oaks and the magnolias and the pines. Then there's the Health and Wellness Center. Most all of us will graduate to a bed there someday. I overheard my smart-aleck grandson calling it the Death Star. He thinks I can't hear through all his teenage mumblings.

At one thirty I start shuffling toward the dining room for my lunch. I go late by design; by now it should be mostly empty and they'll be able to give me a table by myself. As I'm walking I pass other residents who are heading back to their apartments holding styrofoam clamshells of leftovers. They say hello to me and I say hello to them. A lot of them somehow know my name already, but I still don't know but three or four of theirs.

I'm turning the corner when I hear that loudmouth Professor Winston coming my way. I met him at lunch on my second day here. Right now he's leading a pack of about ten biddies and I just catch the tail end of his story. He's saying, "I called the boy into my office at LSU and told him he'd never make a lawyer—twenty-five years later his name's on the ballot and I'm voting for him." The ladies trailing after him cackle and laugh. "So that shows what I know!" he says.

Here the hallway widens into a sitting room and so I step aside to let them all pass. The professor is wearing a cream linen suit and holding a straw boater. He lifts the hat to his ear when he sees me and gives it a wobble. "Good afternoon, June," he says, and I hear two or three of the ladies give little clucks.

"Good day to you all as well," I say. The *you all* catches in my throat and I almost say *y'all.* I've been living outside the piney woods of Mississippi for more than sixty years now, but that still trips me up on occasion. There's the common words I think and the proper words I say. Sometimes they collide in my throat. It's been that way ever since I left home.

The professor stops and smiles at me. He has a full head of silver hair that he brushes straight back from his forehead. The locks flow in waves all the way down to his stiff shirt collar. "When will you be joining us at our table for lunch again?" he asks me. "We'd love to have you."

Patience told me that his wife has been dead almost ten years. Cancer. So I guess he and I got that in common. I've been a widow for fifteen years now.

"Absolutely," drawls one of the women with him. I believe her name is Jeanette. Jeanette Kleinpeter or something.

I'm thinking, *Not never, y'all,* but instead say, "Soon, I hope. I've just been dining so late these days."

The professor grins and starts singing "Soon, June," stretching out both words so that it sounds sort of pretty. So it seems he has a nice voice when he's not lecturing everybody. He heads down the hallway still singing, and beneath his crooning I hear Jeanette whisper to one of the others that she guesses "Miss New Orleans is too good for us Baton Rouge folk."

No, indeed. I've got bad knees and a bad back and a bad heart, but I still have the ears I had when I was a girl in Mississippi. Rabbit, that's what Daddy used to call me. He told me that was his Choctaw name for me.

"Pardon?" I say. "Pardon?" I holler at them pretty good but none of them will turn back and look at me. None save the professor. He stops singing and slows up, but then Jeanette pokes at him with her wrist and so he keeps moving. I swear. Too good for them? On our farm in McComb we had an enormous Nubian goat named Gracie. In the mornings I would milk her, and then I'd hitch up that lop-eared doe to a little wagon and she'd pull me to the schoolhouse. So trust me, I don't think I'm better than anybody. Not in the way Jeanette means, at least.

I'm hot, but I do what I can to put them out of my head and continue on my way. At the end of the hallway I see big Regina standing in front of the entrance to the dining room. She smiles like she's been waiting there just for me. I actually like her okay. She's a cheerful thing, always has a pretty flower of some sort stuck in her hair.

"Well, hello there, Miss June," she says. "How you making out this Saturday?"

"Just fine," I tell her. "Just fine."

"We got your table waiting for you."

"Thank you, Regina."

She touches my periwinkle blouse with her thick fingers. "Boy, that's a pretty silk shirt you wearing today. It's the bluest blue."

I know it's her job to be pleasant, but there's something about the way Regina looks me in the eye that makes me believe it's not all for show. Again I say thank you, then I follow her into the dining room, past the empty tables that are being cleared and reset. Half of them are missing their white tablecloths and so the room has a closed-for-business feel. Regina walks with me to my table by the window and I sit down and glance around. There's no one else in the room except for that quiet man with the gray crewcut and the brown suits. He always comes late and sits alone, just like me. We nod to each other and then we each look out the window. So I guess that's both of our lives now, moving from window to window. Him always in his browns, me always in my blues.

I take a nap after lunch and wake up with my back aching and that same out-of-sorts and hollow feeling I used to get only on Sundays. My apartment has a little bedroom and a little den, a bathroom and a kitchenette. I water my plants and straighten things up—but that doesn't take more than fifteen minutes or so. Our house in Lakewood had two stories and a big backyard. Even with the maid, it still kept me busy. Too busy, according to Selby—and that's the reason I'm here now. I might never see New Orleans again.

The phone rings and I pick it up. It's the guard gate calling. My grandson, Eddie, is stopping by to visit. I can see this out of some book. Give her things to look forward to, but also remember to surprise her from time to time. I want to be difficult but I can't. I love him and I want to see him. "Oh," I say to the man, "go ahead and let him on in, I suppose."

I unlock the sliding glass door in the sunroom and go outside to wait. A wave of hot air hits me like I just opened an oven. There's a parking lot not too far from the pond, and before long Eddie comes pulling in. His vehicle is an embarrassment. I gave him my old beige Cadillac when I moved in here and now he's gone and ruined it—darkened the windows so that I can't even see who's driving, put these hubcaps on the tires that look like chrome sewer lids. Here's a boy who lives in a nice subdivision and goes to a private school. I maneuver all my life to have a grandson like that and now he spends his days wishing he were from some ghetto. But I do love him. He gets out the car and waves to me. "Well, come on," I say. "It's hot out here."

Eddie's wearing jeans that are too big for him and a yellow baseball cap. His white shirt is open at the collar and I can see his gold chain glinting in the sun. Still, when he smiles at me, for a moment I see the straw-haired little boy he once was. "Two seconds," he says. "I got something for you."

He opens the trunk of the Cadillac and takes out a brown paper bag. This ought to be good and special. He needs to shave, and so his pale face looks like it has dirt on it. I wait for him to finally make his way to me and then give him a kiss on his scratchy cheek. He lifts the paper sack up like it's some kind of trophy. "Hummingbird feeder," he says. "You got a screwdriver here?"

And so for the next half-hour instead of visiting with my grandson I sit in the sunroom while he screws the feeder to the side of the pine tree outside my door. When he's finished I mix some sugar and water in an empty milk jug and he fills the feeder for me. I watch him from the doorway. "So are you going to come by and fill that for me every week?" I ask.

Eddie starts to hem and haw because of course he hadn't thought of that when he picked out his present. "Should I put it down lower on the tree?" he asks.

Just then there's a knock at the front door and that saves him.

"I'm teasing you," I tell him. "I can manage fine." I squeeze his skinny arm. "It's wonderful. Thank you."

The knock is Patience coming to check my blood pressure again. I introduce her to my grandson. "Have you met Patience yet, Eddie?"

Eddie comes around my coffee table with his arm stretched out. "What's up?" he says.

Patience shakes his hand and says hello. I can see her sizing up his clothes with her pretty almond eyes. The corner of her mouth twitches and I think she's trying not to laugh. "That's so sweet of you to come by and visit," she tells him.

"It's no thing," says Eddie. He puts his hands flat together and points to the door like he's diving. "But I sort of need to get going now, June."

Patience's eyebrows give a bounce when he says my name. She looks at me, but I just smile. I've made Eddie call me that since day one. I wasn't ever interested in being a Granny or a Gram, a Nana or a Me-maw or Maw-maw.

"Come on now," I say. "Let me get you something cold to drink."

"No, really," says Eddie. "There's some things I gotta do today."

It's a lost cause and I'm not going to beg. "Well, thank you for the hummingbird feeder," I tell him.

"That's no problem," says Eddie.

There's a silence but Patience breaks it. "He got you a bird feeder?" She takes me by the hand. "Well, come on and show me." We all three move to the sunroom and Patience says, "Oh, how nice," when she sees the red feeder screwed to the side of the pine tree. "Aren't you a good grandson," she says to Eddie. Patience is only five or six years older than he is, but I like the way she talks a little bit down to him. I see too many adults trying to be kids these days.

Eddie's looking more and more antsy and now I'm getting annoyed. "Well, get going," I tell him. "I don't want you to fall behind on things." I cross my arms together and he kisses me goodbye.

"I'll stop by and see you again real soon," he says.

"You coming to the picnic tomorrow?"

Eddie weaves his head like a snake. "I don't think I can make that," he says. "But I'll be around here plenty."

"You had better." Seeing him about to go has cooled me back down. "I love you," I tell him. "I love you with all my heart."

"I know," he says. "I love you too."

Eddie tells Patience goodbye and leaves out the door. I see he's got my screwdriver stuffed in his back pocket, but I don't say anything. He'll find it later and maybe it will eat at him until he finally brings it on back to me. These are the games that I'm reduced to playing. Patience closes the door for me, and we stand together in the sunroom watching Eddie walk away. He's skirting the pond when he bends down to pick up a pinecone. He throws it out past the lily pads and it lands with a splash. A little slate heron that I never saw land goes flying off from the cattails and then a car horn honks. One of the black windows rolls down in my old Cadillac, and even through the glass of the sunroom, my rabbit ears hear a girl shout, Eddie, hurry up.

"There's someone waiting in there," I say.

Patience rubs my back with the flat of her hand. "That's *his* car?"

The girl hollers once more and I put my fingers up against the glass. "Why would he just leave somebody in there?"

We get one meal credit per day here at Witness Oaks. They tell me that anything after that will show up on my monthly bill. So I guess, for all her sweetness, Regina is still keeping tabs on us. That's another reason I've started to take my lunch late. When suppertime comes around I usually get by fine with a sandwich or some leftovers, then I walk over to the little bar down the hall for a drink before bed.

I once read somewhere that people are no different from animals in that we also follow regular patterns—rhythms that we rarely deviate from in any meaningful way. I've been thinking about that a lot lately. Take me. I spent the first eighteen years of my life in the piney woods outside McComb, Mississippi, wandering from chores to school to church—and I might have kept at that pattern my whole life if the war hadn't come along. I had a girlfriend who passed the summer visiting family down in New Orleans. Margaret came back in the fall with stories of USO halls and handsome boys who could actually dance—even though we ourselves could not. And there was work to be found, she told me. A girl could start a whole new life in that city. Margaret said that in a few weeks she would begin classes at the secretarial college there. Come on with me, she begged. We can share a room at my auntie's.

And so I went to see Daddy. For reasons I can only guess at, he and Mama never had any children after me. I told him what I was thinking, and he smiled and called me Rabbit. "You always got your ear to the ground," he said. "If New Orleans is shouting for you, then it's shouting for you." Within the year Mama finally died from the quiet come-and-go sickness that had been ailing her all her life. Daddy followed her only a month or so later. Heart attack. I still cry when I think about him. My daddy was my eyes.

I wasn't in New Orleans one week before I met Jack Hopkins. August 7, 1943. It was a Saturday night and we were at the USO on South Rampart Street. Margaret was making a fool out of herself on the dance floor, and I was standing over by the punch bowl in a cheap cotton dress, feeling as country as a dog under a porch. This was the first and only USO dance I would ever go to. It was very crowded and very hot, and the entire place smelled like Picayune cigarettes, Vitalis, and sweat. They must have had twenty black men up on stage, and the jazz that came squalling out of their horns was so loud and relentless that it scared me. Before long I'd had enough. I was walking out just as Jack was walking in. He was an officer, even I could tell that. He held the door open for me and I flat froze for a second. He was slick-haired and broad-shouldered—the best-looking man I ever saw, before or since. I know old folks are always saying things like that, but I really mean it with Jack. He was a few years older than me, and among all those drunk and frightened boys, I thought to myself that here, at last, was a man. I smiled and he smiled and then I hurried to the sidewalk and took a deep breath of that syrupy New Orleans air. I hadn't even exhaled yet when I heard his dress shoes come a-clicking down the steps.

We became a steady couple. Jack was from New Orleans and had been lucky enough to be stationed right up the river at Camp Plauche. Before he shipped out that January he introduced me to his family. They were rich—I found that out soon enough. Jack parked his Chevrolet in front of their big house in the Garden District and I began to cry. He had to tell me a hundred times just how much his parents were going to love me before I finally fixed my makeup and went on inside with him.

And against all odds they did love me—especially his beautiful mother. That Christmas I promised Jack I would wait for him, and all of a sudden my whole life changed. I never worked the first day as a secretary. Jack moved me out of the room I was sharing with Margaret off North Carrollton, and his parents made a place for me in their home. Three weeks before Jack set sail for the Pacific, his mother sat down on the bed with me, started giving me my first lessons on how to act and how to be. "This will be harder on you than on Jack," she told me. "Write him every day, but you also need to try and concentrate on other things while he's gone."

"I'll do my best, ma'am."

"Call me Annie now, okay?"

"Really?"

She smiled and touched my hair. In those days it was the color of honey. "Well," she said, "you certainly are pretty."

"Not half as pretty as you," I said, and I meant it.

"No," said Annie. "Just say thank you when someone pays you a compliment."

"Thank you, then."

"Perfect." Annie pulled me closer to her. "I have always wanted a daughter," she said. "And I suppose that's going to be you, doll."

That night she gave me a blue dress and told me that blue should be my color because it matched my aqua eyes. I was wearing that same dress when Jack came home from the Philippines two years later, his skin so yellow from malaria pills that I hardly recognized him. I called out for him and he looked right through me. I said his name again and he focused and came running. He picked me up in one of those spinning Hollywood hugs and I could hear Annie clapping her hands as she watched us. "Junebelle," he was saying, "you're even more beautiful than I remember."

So that was the great adventure of my life—those years between leaving home and marrying Jack. Life was all surprises then. On the train back from my daddy's funeral, Annie talked me into becoming a Catholic, and she kept on teaching me how to dress and eat and talk. One day the two of us would be walking on Canal Street loaded down with shopping bags and hatboxes, and the next we'd be dining at Galatoire's or Commander's after Mass. After Jack and I married, he took a job with his father and we bought the house in Lakewood. I had Selby and then we tried for a boy but finally quit just like my own parents had. We had a fine life together until one Sunday in November. We were watching the Saints game when four decades of cigarettes came knocking. Jack began coughing blood and in six months he was dead. That was 1990.

Life with Jack was one pattern that I was sorry to see go.

How I spent the next fifteen years isn't really worth talking about. It's five o'clock now. I put on some nice shoes and start walking to the bar.

The bartender is an old black man named Lionel. He sees me coming down the hall and smiles. "Good evening now, Miss June," he says.

"Good evening, Lionel."

Eddie calls this place the Broken Hip. That one actually made me laugh. Its proper name is the Magnolia Lounge. The room has three tables and a rosewood bar with four stools and a brass rail.

Lionel has his hands flat on the bar like he's standing at the controls of a ship. "Can I make you a sazerac?" he asks.

"That would be splendid," I tell him. "Thank you."

Lionel told me that two years ago his kids moved him up to Baton Rouge same as my Selby did me. He swears that he remembers me from when he used to work the Sazerac Bar in the Roosevelt Hotel, way back before it became the Fairmont. He's old enough to be living at Witness Oaks himself, so I take all his memories with a pinch of salt. Still, every evening he reminds me that he remembers me, and because I like to hear that, I always order a sazerac rather than one of the gin martinis that I prefer these days.

"Miss June," he says to me now, "ain't it funny where life takes us?"

"It is indeed, Lionel." I sit down at one of the tables. It's empty in here. It's almost always empty in here.

Lionel takes his time with the sazerac, but that's fine with me because some drinks are meant to take some time in fixing, and besides, when you're only having one, it's nice for there to be a ritual surrounding it. When he finally sets the glass down in front of me I have company in the Magnolia Lounge. The quiet man with the gray crewcut I see most days at lunch has walked up to the bar and ordered a beer. He makes as if to climb onto one of the stools, but then I guess he thinks better of it and goes and sits by himself at a table. This is a small room, more of a closet than a lounge, and if my arm were just a bit longer I could reach out and touch the man on his shoulder. As far as I can tell, he's wearing the same brown suit he had on at lunch today, and up close I can see that it's pretty cheaply made, a suit you might buy off the rack at Penney's. He looks over at me and smiles a sad little smile. I take a sip of my drink and look away. I don't want him ruining this moment for me, this split second when the rye and the bitters hit my throat and I'm reminded of the Roosevelt. Of velvet couches and white gloves, folks fresh off the train having drinks while bellboys haul all their bags up-stairs. I get one second of that before the ice starts to melt and the drink just tastes like licorice—which, as they say, is the way with everything.

I take a few more sips before I realize that the man is cry-ing. Not bawling or anything, just a quiet sucking of air that I'm sure nobody would hear but me. It's not my business but I glance over at him again. The man looks fine to the eye but I know better. He has his beer bottle cradled in his big hands, and he's picking at the red and white label with a blunt finger. There's a gold band wedged tight up against his knuckle. That doesn't really mean anything, though. This place is full of mar-tyrs. Not me. Selby wears my ring.

"Are you all right?" I didn't think I wanted to talk but I guess maybe I do.

The man looks up at me. "What do you mean?" he asks. "I'm doing fine."

He has a country drawl that reminds me of Daddy's. "Where you from?" I ask him.

"Haughton," he says. "Up in north Louisiana." He swaps the *s* in *Louisiana* for a *z* and drops the second syllable, and again I'm reminded of my dead father. I can hear him at the train station seeing me and Margaret off. "Y'all girls be careful in *Looziana*," he'd told us.

"My name's June," I say. "I grew up in Mississippi myself." I don't know why I tell him that. I haven't volunteered that information in ages.

"I'm Bud Long," says the man.

I think again of the Roosevelt, of Earl Long sweeping through the lobby in seersucker. He pinched me on my bottom once and Jack tried to fight him. I ask Bud Long if he's any relation.

"Nope," he says. "None."

"I bet you get that a lot."

"I used to. That's true enough."

He doesn't seem too keen to talk so I focus back on my drink. There are Audubon prints on the walls in here. Paintings of weasels and panthers and deer. I never knew till I came to Witness Oaks that Audubon had painted anything but birds. A chair drags on the hardwood floor and I see Bud Long stand up.

"Good night, June," he says. "It was very nice to have met you, and I thank you for saying hello."

I say goodbye myself and watch him leave. I'm thinking, *Good heavens, that man drinks fasts,* when I look closer at his beer bottle and see that he never took the first sip. That makes me so mad that I holler at him same as I did Jeanette Kleinpeter. "Hey, you," I say. "Bud."

Bud Long turns around. With his gray crewcut he looks like a retired astronaut—and a broken one at that, one who's just been told that he's too old to make the moon shot. "Yes?" he says.

"You got something against sitting next to me and drinking your beer? Do I bother you?" I see Lionel spin around behind the bar when I say that. His back is facing us now, and I guess that's the best he can do to give us some privacy in this tiny place.

Bud looks from me to his beer and back again. The confusion leaves his face and he smiles. "No," he says. "It's not that at all."

"Something funny, Mr. Long?"

"No," he says again. "It's just that I haven't had a drink in thirty years." He scratches his head and looks down at his feet. My old astronaut has turned into a shy paperboy. "So when I thanked you for saying hello," he says, "I really, really meant it."

Bud Long leaves after he says that. Lionel turns back around, and the way he looks at me makes me think he can tell that I feel as small as one of those Audubon squirrels running circles on the wall. I don't know when I started being this mean.

In the morning Patience comes for her measurements. I'm sitting in my sunroom armchair, and she settles onto a little stool beside me. She reminds me that this is the day of the picnic, then sticks the stethoscope in her ears. I don't need to be reminded but people don't seem willing to believe that. Selby called twice last night to tell me one last time that she was coming. She does that now as well—tells me things over and over and over. She wanted me to go to St. Joseph's with her this morning but I begged off. Truth is, I don't believe in a God anymore, Catholic or otherwise. I just woke up the other day and stopped, decided that I wouldn't be saying my morning prayers for once. I thought I'd be sad, but to be honest, it felt delicious. Like that was the last decision I had left that I could make for myself. Who knows? Maybe tomorrow I'll go on back to believing.

Patience writes my blood pressure down on her clipboard and clucks her tongue.

"Well?" I ask.

"You keep on surprising me," she says.

She pulls the cuff from my arm and clips the stethoscope around her slender neck. I'm in a playful mood because my daughter is coming. "You should see me fish," I tell her.

Patience's head snaps up and I give her a wink. She laughs long and hard and I can see on her face a sort of shifting, a look not so different from the one Jack gave me when he saw me helping his mother polish her Dresden china his first Easter back from the war. It's a look that says, Why, Junebelle, maybe I've had you figured all wrong. Patience puts her hand on my arm. "I'm so sorry I ever asked you about fishing," she says.

"Don't be sorry at all," I say. "There was actually a time when I liked to fish very, very much."

Patience is laughing again. "Okay," she says. "I know you're fooling with me." She slaps at my armchair with the limp cuff, then starts to get up.

"Wait one second. There's somebody I want to ask you about."

"All right," says Patience.

"Bud Long."

"Oh, that poor man," says Patience. "They just moved Mrs. Long into Health and Wellness last week."

The picnic begins at eleven o'clock, but by fifteen after Selby still hasn't come and so I leave my apartment without her. I've got on white shoes and a pretty blue dress, and both are altogether silly to wear to a picnic in July. Annie had a hundred different names for the color blue. She would have called this dress cornflower.

The picnic is on a flat lawn set apart from the main buildings. I walk past the pond to the sidewalk, and a bass swirls off from the shallows and heads for deeper waters. A staff member in a golf cart sees me walking and asks if I would like a ride. My knees are throbbing but I tell him no, that I believe I can make it on my own. My shoes sound like goat hooves on the concrete.

When I come around the corner I realize pretty quickly that this picnic is a much larger operation than I had imagined it would be. A big white shade tent went up sometime during the night, and in every corner there's a tall box fan blowing on an enormous block of ice. In the distance I can hear the faint hum of the generators fighting to keep everyone cool.

Already the tent is crowded. There are ten rows of tables, but no seats where I can go off and be by myself. Everybody is sitting but me, and since no food's been served yet they look like they all just came here to wait for something. I can feel everyone watching me in my blue dress and so I keep walking. I walk in one end of that circus tent and out the other. I hear the professor calling my name as I go by. "Sit with us, June," he says. A hand touches my arm but I don't break my stride. I squeeze past a fan and make it outside. Free.

There's a smaller tent set up in the corner of the clipped-grass lawn, just a little red tarp to beat back the sun. Smoke is pouring out from a stacked pile of cinder blocks, and four of the black men from the kitchen are standing under the tarp shooting the breeze. I can smell the hog cooking. The men catch me sniffing and they all four wave. They look tired and I'm guessing that they've been at this since yesterday. One of them takes a step toward me. His skin is shiny with sweat. "You wanna come and see, ma'am?" he asks. "It's near about done."

I'm curious but I shake my head. Right now I only want to

go to a place where people can't stare at me. I walk across the lawn toward the big live oak looming at the far end. Its lower branches have grown so thick and heavy and tired that they lie along the ground like fat snakes. This is one of the witness trees that gave this place its name. The retirement home's literature claims that the old oaks sprinkled across these fifty acres have seen French soldiers and Spanish soldiers and British soldiers, Billy Yanks and Johnny Rebs. I get what they're suggesting—that us old folks are like these dying trees. Bravo.

My eyes haven't kept quite like my ears, and I don't see Bud Long until I'm already standing beneath the canopy of the oak. It's dim under here, and wide limbs are twisting this way and that. The ground all around me has not seen good sun in a hundred years, and instead of grass there's only dust-fine dirt. Bud Long is sitting by himself on one of the earthbound tree limbs. He has a green can of soda in his hand and is watching me.

"Hello," he says.

"Hey there," I say.

He's wearing a brown suit but I think it's a different one today. His jacket is folded beside him, and his wide striped tie and short-sleeve shirt match his NASA hair. He looks like he just walked here straight from Mission Control. He pats the jacket with his hand. "Wanna sit down?" he asks.

"I'm not really up for talking," I tell him.

"That's fine," he says. "I ain't neither."

And so with that understanding between us I do go ahead and sit beside him. His jacket protects my cornflower dress from the dirty bark and I'm comfortable here. Bud Long has another cold drink sweating beside him, and he pops it open and hands it to me. I thank him and we shut up.

It's nice and cool beneath the tree, and I can hear all different things at once with my uncommon ears: the droning of the generators and the murmur of the old folks, the laughter of the cooks with their hog. Sitting beneath that tree I feel like Bud and me can watch the world but it can't watch us. Through the tangle of the oak branches I spot Patience come walking out of the tent with my family. I see Selby with her husband and remember when that man was just a boy on my doorstep. And then my grandson comes slouching out behind them. Eddie and his gold chain have made it after all. Patience hollers to the cooks and they point toward us and holler back. Before long they'll have found me, and so I sit with Bud and we wait, watching them all come on.

Bluebonnet Swamp

BLUEBONNET SWAMP is a swamp in miniature. Sixty, seventy acres of cypress and tupelo set aside within the city. Baton Rouge drains into the swamp, and the swamp seeps into the earth.

A trail leads from the nature center into the low, wet hardwoods, then gives way to a boardwalk that skirts the refuge and dead-ends at the library. Here an office park borders the swamp. At night raccoons scale the hog-wire fence separating the two worlds; they thieve and plunder trash.

His law office looks out over the petite swamp, and the first time he sees her is on a Tuesday, strolling the boardwalk in a pale blue dress.

Wednesday afternoon, he sees her again. He is staring out his window when she appears. She catches him watching and gives a low half wave. She is light-haired, small, and pretty. She smiles and then she is gone.

Thursday, she comes. Friday, she comes. Always alone, always in that robin's egg dress.

How odd, he thinks, how sad—this woman who walks alone in a steaming summer swamp. If he sees her on Monday, he will speak with her.

. . .

Bluebonnet Swamp is too small for deer, though on rare occasions there are tracks that cannot be explained other than to say deer sometimes travel great distances with a full moon.

A queen bobcat lives in the hollow base of a dead cypress; every spring a male finds her and they become a pair, then she bears a litter that the tom picks off one by one because he is always hungry and because the thin city swamp could never support more than two bobcats.

In the fall, wood ducks swim among the water oaks and dabble-dive for acorns, but now it is summer, and the swamp is drought-dry, save for occasional puddles into which the moccasins have retreated, as well as a couple of chicken gators that are like tiny earthbound dragons dreaming of rich saltwater marshes they will never see.

Two of his law partners visit over the weekend, dropping by unannounced on their way home from the golf course. They drink gin and tonics on his back patio, then get to the point.

Don't take this wrong, we're one hundred percent behind you—but it's been six months now and your hours are still slacking.

He winces, but they continue.

Look, we know losing her is something you will never really get over—God knows, we all just loved her—but we're also running a business. You need to pick up the pace.

I understand, he says. He shows them to the door then, later, buries his face in the nightgown that still smells of her and falls asleep crying.

He goes into work on Sunday morning and tries to ignore the woman in blue who has been watching him from the end of the boardwalk since dawn. An hour and he gives up. He slips out the back door of his office and moves toward her.

She smiles as he climbs the briar-choked fence and then helps pull him up onto the boardwalk. He says hello and she turns and leads him back the way she came, into the swamp.

They leave the boardwalk and the first thing she shows him is a Burmese python, an escaped pet gone feral. The thick, mottled snake is stretched ten feet across a sun-dappled clearing. It senses their approach with a tongue flick.

The great trick to a snake's life, she tells him, is to absorb enough daylight to survive the night. The python will last the summer—hunt bullfrogs and rabbits and eat well, live well—but in the end it will die because fall always comes and a jungle snake just can't tolerate more than a few cool nights.

They quit the sleeping, doomed python, and she takes him to a place where the swamp rises into magnolia-beech upland. The small hillside is crumbling, and a cave has formed beneath the undercut base of a live oak. I know this place, he tells her. When I was a boy, we lived not too far away. I was alone a lot and so I roamed this swamp. The mud cave was here even then. He kneels and peers into the darkness. I wanted to explore it so badly, he says, just knew it would lead to some other world.

So why didn't you? she asks.

I was afraid, he says, figured the earth would collapse behind me and trap me, bury me alive.

She touches him, takes his hand. He gives himself to her and though it is dark at first, a few steps more and he can't believe what he is seeing, what he has been missing this whole time, these worlds within worlds.

The Final Conner

A TRAIN CROWDED with summer tourists takes Ellis from the airport into Amsterdam. He finds a hotel near the main station and checks his small bag. He's dead tired but fights to stay awake until dark. Keep moving, he tells himself. That's the only way he knows to beat the jet lag.

Tomorrow he will drive into Germany and start making his way to Volkstadt, home of his grandfather's grave. But first this lonely and out-of-the-way stop—not in Bremen or Hamburg or Hanover, but here. He's been in Amsterdam once before, passed through with Amy on their honeymoon a decade ago. His marriage might very well be over but he's right back where they started, albeit alone. All he can figure is that he is here now because he is a poet, and it is in the nature of poets to torture themselves.

Amsterdam seems pretty much the same as he left it—low-slung, watery, and gray. The air is cool and moist, sea air that he drinks in great gulps as he wanders toward the red-light district. At a McDonald's he stops and buys a cup of weak coffee. A block down, a bridge passes over a nice stretch of water. He's halfway across when he realizes whores are watching him from either side of the canal. Ellis catches a déjà vu feeling. He and Amy once had a little argument over him calling these window girls whores. "You have a misogynist streak you need to work on," she had told him, smiling but serious.

"What would you have me call them?"

"Prostituted women."

"But that's such a cold term." Ellis laughed. "You're every ounce the lawyer."

"So sorry if it's not poetic enough for you."

"Well, it's not."

"Forget it. I wasn't trying to start a fight."

And this had been their honeymoon.

The closest of the women taps at her window as Ellis daydreams. He glances over and regards the big African. Her eyes roll back like a feeding shark's and she bobs her head, her mouth an empty cave as she signs for his business. Ellis watches her. It's bright day, barely past lunchtime. Her head moves faster and faster, up and down, up and down. She thinks she has him on the hook, just needs to reel him on in. Maybe she does, he admits. He really hasn't been himself lately.

The African rises from her stool and presses herself flat against the glass. She is dancing for him when an older man steps between them. The man pushes on her door and enters the tiny room. Ellis winces and the woman gives him a maybe-later shrug of her shoulders. She snaps the red curtain shut, and he stands there drinking his McDonald's coffee. Ellis imagines the two of them behind that dirty pane of glass, that thin red curtain. Christ, the things that go on behind closed doors.

In 1945, Ellis's grandfather was shot down over northern Germany and his body was never recovered. The hero pilot's young son grew up to become an aloof, distant father to Ellis, then took his own life when Ellis was five years old. The only vivid memory Ellis has of him is from the night he died, an evening spent fishing the bay bridge near their home in Pensacola. They brought home a sand shark that the sad man butchered in the garage. He told Ellis to bury the head in a backyard ant pile and promised that later, together, they would bleach out the jaws.

His mother dressed him just like a little man for the funeral. Afterward, his house packed full of strangers, Ellis remembered the sand shark and slipped out the door. He wandered the yard in his new clothes only to find the nest raided and the head missing, stolen by neighborhood coons. Their thin-fingered tracks led off a few yards before disappearing into the thick, dry Bermuda.

Thirty-one summers later, Ellis had been night-fishing his father's favorite spot on the old Highway 98 bridge when Amy surprised him at his setup. She said she couldn't sleep. She could never sleep after they fought. Neither one of them could.

"I'm sorry," Ellis told her. "I shouldn't have said all the things I said."

Amy folded her arms and sat on the concrete railing of the bridge. Her auburn hair was tucked under a baseball hat, but a few here-and-there strands had worked loose and were wisping in the salt breeze. "Like when you told me I don't know you at all?" she asked.

"Yes," said Ellis. "I think now that I've just changed. I remember being happier."

"With me?"

"Happier with myself, I mean."

Amy nodded but kept quiet, and so Ellis tied a halogen lamp to a length of nylon rope and lowered it from the railing. The lamp hung suspended over the black water of the bay like a setting sun. Amy leaned over the side of the bridge with him and they watched shrimp flea-skip to the light. He rigged another pole as trout began to feed—mostly whites, but some specks. Together they filled an ice chest.

Ellis cleaned the fish on the railing and Amy shared her hot tea, offered some of the mandel bread she had made to calm herself after their fight. It looked delicious but he refused. The mandel bread, the old Mets hat she wore so well—on that night those things only saddened him, served to remind him that his wife had left almost everything she knew to follow him from Manhattan to Pensacola. He thought back to a poetry reading in the Village long ago. They'd been in a candlelit basement bar somewhere in the Village, would never love each other more than they did at that moment. In a month he would be finished at NYU. "I'm sorry, but my heart," he had told her, "belongs in the Panhandle." She had teased him about that for years.

"It's funny," said Amy on the bridge, her voice small in the night, "the shrimp you use for bait aren't kosher"—she brought her hands together and smiled—"but the trout are."

The idea of converting something forbidden and cursed into something useful and blessed—he could tell that this appealed to her. Ellis looked up and saw that she was staring at the bone moon. She looked tired. He loved his wife but knew that he had failed her in nearly every way, large and small, that a man could fail a woman.

"I'm just not ready for kids," he said. "Truth is, I'm not sure I ever will be."

Amy nodded and asked him to move out, maybe for a month, maybe longer.

"So maybe forever?" asked Ellis.

"Yes," she said. "Maybe forever."

The following week she helped him pack. He wanted to take along the extra coffeemaker and so she disappeared into the attic. Before long she returned carrying a small cedar chest. "I found this," she said. "It was buried under some blankets."

"What is it?"

"I don't really know," she said. "Old stuff."

Amy handed him the chest and inside he found an American flag and a Purple Heart, old letters bound by ribbon and yellow with age, a black-and-white photograph of a memorial headstone in Arlington. These were his grandmother's things, things Ellis hadn't known he owned but that had somehow, some way, followed him all these years.

"I thought you might want to go through it all sometime," she said, and then she turned to go back up and look for the coffeemaker.

This thoughtfulness, this effortless and persisting kindness, was typical of her. He felt his heart break just a little more as she left him holding the chest.

Ellis explores Amsterdam until dark, then crashes at the hotel and sleeps until his eleven o'clock checkout. After breakfast he walks to the train station, rents a tiny red Fiat, and leaves the city behind. His passenger seat is plastered with Google maps; Volkstadt is only four or five hours away. He tackles the countryside, the nether Netherlands.

At midday he enters Germany. He pushes east until he crosses the Weser River and then aims for the North Sea. In the afternoon he arrives in a pretty port town named Cuxhaven. He stops here and walks the beach, sees that the tide is gone. The shallow bay has been laid bare, and the ocean floor is a naked field of compact mud. Tourists wander the bubbling mud flat as a line of ponies slogs north, carrying riders to a barrier island in the hazy distance some five, six miles off. Must be something, Ellis thinks, riding out to an island, shooting a low-tide window. How safe that would feel: to be high and dry at the end of the day, brushing down your tired horse as the sea closes in behind you.

Volkstadt is just down the road. Ellis has a few hours of daylight and figures he could make it still—but he's not ready to leave quite yet. Pastor Weis isn't expecting him until tomorrow, and besides, this shouldn't come too easily.

Amy would like this place, he decides, this place where the ocean simply disappears, vanishes twice a day. Ellis checks in to a hotel near the beach and thinks of her, watches from his window as families and lovers return from the empty bay, racing to beat that same tide they'd once chased.

After the split Ellis moved into a furnished, second-chance apartment near I-10. From the balcony of his new home, he could glimpse just a sliver of Escambia Bay. His first day at the Gulf Winds Suites, he watched a sailboat slide across his pie slice of water. The landlady told him that he was lucky as she pressed a key into his hand—month-to-month rentals are low priority, these units typically face the interstate. The sailboat disappeared and he felt less than lucky.

A stocky man was smoking a cigar in the sweltering parking lot, a white towel draped over his bald head. He spotted Ellis unloading his dying Taurus and shuffled over, asked if he needed a hand. Ellis didn't have much but the stranger wouldn't take no. "Name's Frank Thaxter." The sweaty man grabbed the heaviest suitcase. "Lead the way." Two trips and they were done.

Frank was about fifty and retired army—in at eighteen, out at thirty-eight—now he ran a small pressure-washing business just to stay busy. Ellis told him that he taught in the English department at West Florida. Frank pressed and Ellis explained that he taught poetry. That he was, in fact, a poet.

"Hey, like Shakespeare?"

"Sure, yeah, I like Shakespeare."

"No, I mean you're a poet, a poet like Shakespeare?"

"Exactly like Shakespeare," said Ellis. "Maybe better."

"Are you famous?"

Ellis shook his head. "There are no famous poets anymore, not really."

"Sure there are."

"Name me one."

Frank shrugged and invited him for beers but Ellis begged off, said he needed to go and wash up.

"Wash up?"

"Yeah," said Ellis.

Frank slapped him on the back. "I'll give you an hour, Shakespeare. Meet me outside at seventeen hundred."

Frank left before Ellis could form another excuse. The door closed and Ellis glanced out the window. Overhead a plane crossed the big blue sky, pulling a long banner from some pine-woods airport south to Pensacola Beach. He stood there and read about happy hour—dollar Long Islands and two-for-one Jell-O shots at some bar he'd never even heard of.

Ellis sat down with his notebook at the small table in the kitchen. He was still considering the sailboat and thought that maybe there was a poem there—poetry in the sadness of a man staring out at his own cut corner of the sea. A man watching, waiting, hoping for beauty to pass on by, afraid that if he looks away he'll miss something special. Ellis compared the sailboat to a butterfly: a monarch carried across a tide pool, teased by a clear current.

Even as Ellis wrote he knew that it was all wrong, that he'd used this before. The floating-butterfly-as-a-sailboat met-aphor was buried somewhere in his first collection. Yet again he'd come full circle and plagiarized himself, recycled a senti-mental image that once had come honestly to his younger self. Worlds in tide pools. Christ. If he didn't stop soon she would come—her—the girl from the first stanza of the first poem he ever published. She would have dark hair and skin smooth as

river sand. She'd smell honeysuckle in the tangles / for lone-
liness, there would be a whippoorwill / to suggest movement,
deer, just off the beach, a herd of whitetails easing through the
longleafs in one fluid motion.

Not that it really mattered. He'd been dismissed early on
as a poet of consequence. If he was appreciated at all it was as
a regional voice, the quaint Southern poet, a cartoon of sorts.
Ellis broke his pencil and rose from the table. He went down-
stairs to meet Frank and found him waiting in the parking lot
for his new friend Shakespeare.

The receptionist greets him in English as he checks out of the
hotel in Cuxhaven. He passes her the room key, and she asks
him where he's headed this morning. He tells her Volkstadt,
and she points to a young man in the corner of the lobby. The
man is sitting on a toolbox and dressed in work clothes. The receptionist smiles as she suggests that Ellis might give the *wanderbursche* a ride south.

"*Wanderbursche?*"

"Like an apprentice," she explains. "They travel Germany
and train under different masters."

"Neat," says Ellis. "Cool."

The receptionist studies him. "It is good luck to assist them,"
she says.

Ellis looks over at the *wanderbursche*. He is thin with stringy
brown hair. The man is grinning as if he senses someone might
be about to help him. "No problem," says Ellis at last.

"No problem? Is okay?"

"Is okay."

The receptionist speaks to the *wanderbursche*, and he rises
and shoulders his bag. Ellis shakes his hand and the man follows him out to the car. He is shy but seems pleased by the red
Fiat. He slips inside and immediately falls asleep. That would

be nice, Ellis thinks, to be a *wanderbursche*. To wander, but to wander with some greater purpose, a whole nation looking to play Samaritan and help you on your way.

Frank was a divorcé regular at Hooters and knew all the waitresses. They hadn't even sat before a tanned blonde named Stacey had set them up with a pitcher and two cold glasses. She sat down as she took their order and built the illusion that they were just three great friends—Frank, Stacey, and Ellis—three great friends watching the Braves play over by her house. Wait right here while I get you boys some wings, make yourselves at home.

Ellis recognized one of the girls. She was on the far side of the restaurant and hadn't spotted him yet. Frank told Ellis her name, and he placed her, remembered her from a workshop that she had dropped midsemester, remembered how she had written a sestina that made Amy cry when he read it to her at dinner. Ellis pretended to be watching the baseball game but was really watching the talented redhead. He was wondering whether she still wrote poetry, whether she was now working outside the rigid structures of sonnets and sestinas that he had forced her to learn. Whether she was once again experimenting with free verse and sprung rhythm. It was there, she had told him in a goodbye e-mail, that her heart truly belonged.

After they left, Ellis spun around in the parking lot and looked back at Hooters glowing like a spaceship in the dark night. The poet waitress was watching him from a window, and he gave a little wave. She waved back and smiled to let him know she remembered him. He felt bad for not saying hello. She returned to wiping down her tables and he thought, not for the first time, that you could tell a lot about a society by the way it treated its artists.

· · ·

Alone in his new apartment, Ellis started to set up the coffee-maker but instead poured a scotch from the quarter bottle of Chivas that Frank had insisted he take. He tried Letterman before the dead screen reminded him that the cable hadn't been turned on. With nothing else to do, he carried his grand-mother's chest over to the couch and pulled out the old letters. The delicate blue ribbon fell apart in his hands, and he imagined her tying it for the last time. Grandma Conner. He had met her only once. She drove down from Birmingham for his father's funeral and the scattering of his ashes in the Gulf. She showed up late and never cried—just pinched Ellis for wiggling during the service. A year later, his mother told him that she had passed, slipped on some rare southern ice and broke her mean neck. They both skipped her funeral.

He spread the letters out across the coffee table and read them from beginning to end. They covered just three months, following Claude Conner from flight school to England. He'd been younger than Ellis was now, a boy captain bragging on his plane and his buddies, promising his pregnant wife that they had the Germans on the run. He'd named his fighter 'Bama Belle, let his best girl know just how much he missed her.

Ellis tried to picture his angry grandmother as a young woman, as a person who deserved such words. There was something his mother had told him when the Alzheimer's was tipping her hidden cards, back before it stole her deck. "Grandma Conner was horrible to your father," she had whispered. "That woman did not have a good life."

The thought that all lives are not equal. That a person could simply *have a bad life*. Ellis shook his head. You spend a lifetime living, your allotted years of loving, laughing, and struggling, then someone comes along and weighs it all out for you, sums it up in a sentence—a good life versus a bad life. At what point is the die cast? At what point does it become too late to salvage a life, pointless to even try?

He was returning his grandfather's letters to the chest when he spotted a single envelope hidden within the folds of the American flag. The stationery was different but, like the others, was addressed to his grandmother in Alabama. Ellis studied the postmark, saw that it was German and dated 1946. Two sheets of paper were tucked inside. He flattened the first out on his thigh and deciphered the shaky script:

> Ness,
> My plane went down and I believe that this is it for me. I will love you always. Remember that—Always.
>   Claude, Your Husband

The second sheet was without salutation or signature, just three paragraphs of neat German. Ellis turned over both pages in his hands but there was nothing more. He sat back on the couch and sipped the last of his scotch, pondered the letter until he fell asleep holding an empty glass.

On the outskirts of Volkstadt, the *wanderbursche* taps the dashboard. Ellis pulls over and wishes him all the best, then leaves the young man standing at the roundabout intersection of two country roads. Alone again, he does three or four circles in the Fiat. The *wanderbursche* is doubled over laughing like a silent-film actor when Ellis finally breaks his comic orbit and continues on his way.

He can see the town in the distance and then, there, a steeple rising above fields of cut hay and feed corn. St. Sebastian. Ellis parks at the quiet church and walks a path that leads around back. There is a cemetery here, a neat acre. He wanders the rows searching tombstones until, on the fifth row, he finds him.

The grave is framed by a rectangle of smooth stones. Inside,

the black dirt has been raked level and freshly planted with ge-
raniums: pretty reds, whites, and blues. Ellis runs his fingers
across the small granite marker, the Christian cross, the three
short lines:

C.C.

VERM. IM OSTEN

1922–1945

The air is clean and the green grass soft, that lush summer
grass you find in places that collect heavy snow in winter. Ellis is about to sit down when he sees a man enter the cemetery
and begin walking toward him.

His first morning in the Gulf Winds Suites, Ellis woke early and
spent an hour on his poetry. For writing, the apartment was
perfect—spare and without distraction, silent save for the distant, white-noise hum of traffic on the interstate. Still, he could
not finish a line. There was no flow; there was no rhythm. He
could think only of the letter and so he took it out, stared at the
German words as if something might click, as if the consonants
and vowels might reshuffle on the page, reveal their meaning
following some mad, magic scramble.

He took a walk to clear his head and found Frank in the
parking lot loading equipment into the back of his truck. They
talked awhile then Ellis mentioned the letter, told Frank that
he might head over to the bookstore and pick up a German-to-
English dictionary.

"Hey, don't bother," said Frank. "My partner, Johnny, served
three years in K-town. He can speak German like the goddamn
kaiser."

"Partner?"

Frank punched him in the shoulder. "Business partner. We
spray houses together."

"No kidding?"

"Like the goddamn kaiser," Frank repeated. "He should be here any minute."

"Good enough." Ellis flipped a five-gallon bucket and watched Frank mix gas. After a short while an old white van pulled up, PATRIOTIC PRESSURE WASHING spelled out on the hood in shiny mailbox letters. The driver was a tall, thin black man who looked about Frank's age. He strode over and Frank introduced him to Ellis, said, "Hey, Johnny, hey. We've got a big mystery that needs solving."

Ellis explained to Johnny about the letter and the man nodded as if someone had just told him the same story an hour ago, like he was called in on this sort of thing all the time. Ellis removed the letter from his shirt pocket and read Claude Conner's short goodbye aloud. When he was finished he passed the second sheet to Johnny.

Johnny cleared his throat and started in with the German, reading very slowly as he translated.

On the third of January 1945, your husband's plane crashed into a field near our village. He was very badly injured and died that night in my home, only a short time after writing you.

Please know that we are Christians. We cared for your husband the best we could and brought him no harm. He died bravely and without much pain. I am sorry that we were not able to save him.

The horrible war has finally ended. Many of our own young men never returned home, and you should know where your loved one rests. Our village is Volkstadt, near the North Sea in Lower Saxony. In the cemetery of St. Sebastian Church, there is a tombstone that bears your husband's initials. God bless.

Johnny finished and Frank whistled between his teeth. "Holy shit," he said. "Your grandmother never told anyone about this?"

Ellis shook his head and Johnny handed him back the letter. "You have to bring him home," he said.

"Johnny's right," Frank chimed. "No man left behind."

"Hoo-ah," said Johnny.

"Good God," said Ellis. "Really?"

"Really," they said, answering him in singsong unison.

Pastor Weis is maybe sixty, has gray hair, a gray beard. Ellis stands to meet him and they shake hands. "You must be Ellis," he says. "I saw you from the window of the church." He speaks softly, but Ellis recognizes his stiff English from their phone conversations.

"Yes," says Ellis. "I appreciate all of your help."

"I was glad I could be of assistance." He gives a kind smile. "Will you be arranging to take him back to America?"

"Maybe, I don't know for sure." Ellis points to the flowers covering the grave. "Who keeps this up so nice?"

"I do."

"Thank you for that."

Pastor Weis bows slightly. "Certainly," he says. "I promised that to Pastor Licht before he died. It was very important to him."

He has told Ellis about Licht already. This man had cared for Claude Conner at the end, prayed with him and insisted that he be buried here. Ellis thinks of Frank Thaxter and the *wanderbursche*, of the importance of showing kindness to strangers. "So what does this mean?" Ellis says finally, pointing to the tombstone. "These words?"

"*Vermisst im Osten* was for the soldiers lost in Russia. It means to be missing in the East." He shrugs. "I suppose Pastor Licht felt that it would be fitting for your grandfather as well, so far from his home."

Ellis smiles at the found poetry and says that he thinks so too.

"There is more," says Weis, "some of your grandfather's things."

Ellis was lunching on leftover chicken wings when Amy stopped by to drop off the charger for his cell phone. She was in tennis whites and on her way to the park. New clothes, tennis—this bothered him a great deal. Who was this ponytailed cheerleader drinking Starbucks in his apartment? She turned to leave and Ellis mentioned his grandfather's letter, the note in German.

"That's incredible," she said.

"I know."

"Can I see them?"

Ellis handed her the fragile pages and recited Johnny's translation as best he could remember. Amy listened and then asked for the other letters, curling on the couch like a teenager while she read through them all. She looked beautiful and when she had finished Ellis saw that she was crying. She wiped her eyes and went to him, took his hand and led him to the bedroom.

It had been a long time, a real long time. Ellis held her and she frowned, whispered, "This is a big mistake, mister," even as their lips met. The strange room smelled of carpet freshener and there, there on that rented bed, Ellis wondered whether they were having sex, making love, or doing something else —something that fell in between, something that people did just to wake up empty spaces.

Later, he lay spent as Amy pulled on her skirt. "Your new friends are right," she told him. "You should go to Germany."

"Maybe one day," said Ellis. "There's sort of a lot going on in my life right now."

"But you need to find your grandfather." Amy squeezed his wrist. "I feel that in my bones."

Ellis smiled in the half-light of the windowless room. Amy was one of those people who believed in signs. Their friends made hay out of that, how the attorney was more romantic than the poet. "We'll see," he said, even though, at least in some small way, he knew that she was right—that their marriage didn't stand a chance so long as he was living in the Gulf Winds Suites, shooting the breeze with the boys at Patriotic Pressure Washing.

"You do that, Ellis." Amy tied her new white shoes and sighed. "You wait and see." She left the apartment in a hurry and without saying more, rushed out as if she had already said goodbye. He called for her to come back but she was no longer listening.

Pastor Weis invites him to stay, but Ellis resists and leaves Volkstadt that afternoon. He's wearing a flight jacket now, and in places the old leather is cracking. Dog tags hang from his neck and are cold against his skin.

Ellis searches the jacket as he drives. In one pocket he finds a Zippo lighter and an empty pack of Lucky Strikes. In another he finds a folded sheet of yellowed paper. Ellis pulls over onto the shoulder of the same roundabout intersection where he released the *wanderbursche*. The young man is gone now, off to learn his trade. Ellis flattens the paper out over the steering wheel and kills the engine.

It's a letter from his Grandma Conner. She's telling her husband that she does not love him. That the baby she's carrying belongs to some stateside officer she's gone and fallen for. Her lover will be leaving his wife; they will be getting married; the 'Bama Belle wants a divorce.

After a while Ellis starts the Fiat and drives. He returns to Cuxhaven, parks near the beach, and sheds his shoes. The tide is withdrawing and he walks out onto the mud flat. The mud is like clay, firm and cool beneath his feet. He stops to investigate a shallow pool where sea birds have gathered to worry the remains of some small shark or dogfish. A filthy gull plucks at the rotting carcass with its yellow beak. Ellis looks away and then continues on, leaving the birds to their stabbings.

A man and boy are hiking out to the barrier island, and Ellis falls in behind them. A strong, chill wind blows in from the north. He jams his fists deeper into the pockets of his jeans. The floor of the bay is not as flat as it seems from the beach. There are grooves in the mud that run like shallow rivers. The father and son march on but Ellis soon tires of all the wandering. He sits down amid the tangled delta of channels and thinks about the letter that he found in Captain Conner's cracked leather jacket, a letter that maybe sent the man's P-51 spinning.

Hours pass and Ellis watches fascinated as the North Sea begins its sudden return. The tideways bubble to life, and seawater sloshes at his feet. Frigid creeks form and the flotsam and jetsam of the world begin to pass him on by: feathers and wood, sea grass and shells. He opens his hands and watches the ocean carry off the letter.

And then he'll be damned if he doesn't see a butterfly caught in the rising tide, its tiny legs fighting for purchase. Ellis shivers as he studies his metaphor incarnate. He realizes then that butterflies-on-the-water are nothing at all like peaceful summer sailboats. Adrift, fighting wet wings, a butterfly-on-the-water is a creature in peril, a soft soul dying in earnest. There's no real beauty in that; he was a fool to have ever believed such a lie. He is finally seeing things as they really are. So he's no Conner after all.

Ellis looks to the distant shore. A crowd has gathered; Germans are pointing at him. He places the wet butterfly on his shoulder and stands. The tourists cheer for him as he begins splashing his way back toward them. He crawls exhausted and dripping and cold onto the beach. A brave little boy figures Ellis for the American that he is and approaches, says, "You a very, very lucky, *mein Herr*. Very lucky to be alive."

The Redfish

THE BOSSMAN CALLED late Saturday and offered time-and-a-half cash wages in exchange for Luther's help clearing the dock, a hand moving equipment into the warehouse while the rest of the city evacuated.

Luther agreed to come in, both as a favor to Quinn and because he needed extra money for food and gas, a motel room once they got far enough north. As he expected, Shonda threw a fit—her mama was waiting on them to pick her up in Mississippi—still, in the end, he was able to convince her to hold off on leaving until the next morning. It's like they say, money talks.

He put on his blue work Dickies and waited for Quinn at the edge of the projects, under the streetlight at the corner of Gibson and Senate. He'd been standing there just a few minutes when a couple of teenagers stepped out of the darkness and shuffled over. The smaller of the two boys strutted with the confidence of the armed and dangerous. He presented himself to Luther. "You Redfish?" he asked. "Redfish Jackson?"

Luther nodded slightly as he stared down the empty street, searching for Quinn's truck.

"Oh, fuck! The Redfish!" The boy brought a hand to his mouth like he might sneeze, then spun around to his friend. "I told you it was him!" He turned back to Luther. "How long you been out?"

Luther looked away from the road and locked eyes with the boy. "Nine months," he said.

"No shit?" The boy shook his head. "Man, I ain't seen you once."

Luther shrugged. "I think maybe you and me work different hours."

The boy clapped his small hands and laughed. "Yeah, you right," he said.

Quinn's pickup turned the corner onto Gibson and its headlights flashed three times. Luther stepped out onto the curb but the boy grabbed his wrist, stopping him. "You need money, come see me," he said. "I might be able to use you."

Luther flicked his wrist, breaking the boy's grip, as he climbed into the cab and closed the door. Marvin Gaye crooned from the radio and Quinn grooved along, sang "'Brother, brother, brother'" as he put the truck in gear. Luther's boss scratched the side of his graying beard and stopped singing. "Everything straight?" he asked.

Luther turned and looked back at the boys, the young lions standing alone in the gold glow of the streetlight. "Damn kids," he said. "Wear me out sometimes."

Quinn laughed. "Wait till you get to be my age," he said. "They'll be wearing you out *all the times*."

They worked through the night and were finishing up early Sunday morning when an NOPD cruiser crossed the tracks that ran alongside the Press Street Wharf. A tired officer stepped out and told them the evacuation would be declared mandatory soon enough—the both of them should be getting on the road.

It was the Italian cop Quinn knew from the VFW. Luther

hung back as the two men spoke. Quinn waved a hand in the direction of his warehouse. "All due respect," he said. "I ain't going nowhere."

The cop frowned and glanced over at Luther. He was sizing him up, studying the prison tattoos that ran the lengths of his broad forearms. He spoke to Quinn but his eyes lingered on Luther. "Then I'm supposed to tell you something," he said. "I'm supposed to tell you to write your Social Security number on your chest with a permanent marker."

"That right?" said Quinn.

"That's meant to scare you when I say that. Make you go on and leave."

Quinn grinned. "Shit, Carl. How many sixty-year-old men they got running around this city with a thirteen-inch johnson?"

Luther snorted and the cop shook his head, smiled himself.

"Just the two of us, I suppose."

"Well, there you go," said Quinn. "A black one and a white one. That oughtta be easy enough for them to sort out."

The cop chuckled. "Either way, you boys be careful." He opened the door of his cruiser. "This looks to be the real deal."

They watched the cruiser pull away and then finished clearing the dock. When they were done, Quinn locked the warehouse and drove Luther north back to the St. Bernard Projects. The sun was up but they didn't see many cars until they crossed under the interstate. People were leaving.

Quinn stopped the truck at the same spot on Gibson where he had picked up Luther earlier, then pulled a roll of cash from his front pocket and counted out six twenties. "That fair?" he asked.

"Yeah," said Luther. "Thanks, chief."

"All right then," said Quinn.

"All right then."

"You know, I talked to that lawyer about you again. He still says you might be owed some money for all that time you spent in Angola."

"Yeah?"

"What he says. You wanna talk to him sometime?"

"Maybe. We'll see."

"You said that last time I asked."

"I know."

"So how about you just tell me when you're ready," said Quinn. "Otherwise I won't bring it up no more."

"Thanks," said Luther. "I'll keep thinking on it."

"Later on, son."

Luther stepped out of the truck. A tree grew between the road and the broken sidewalk, a big oak scarred with bullet holes. As a child, Luther would spoon lead from its trunk and lower branches. He patted the tree and began a slow stroll to where the brick tenements began their sprawl. He was dead tired and prayed Shonda would drive the first stretch. "Please, woman," he whispered to himself. "Lemme catch some sleep."

The Friday-afternoon fights had been arranged by a little hunchback named Doyle for his wannabe Mafia friends, slick-haired twentysomethings in expensive leather coats. Luther was one of their favorites. He earned five hundred for fighting, a thousand for winning. You fought until someone either said give, that or was knocked out.

A couple dozen had been on hand to watch Luther take on the Mexican, an enormous day laborer that Doyle found God knows where. The illegal was even bigger than Luther, maybe six-six, three hundred pounds. They took off their shirts and Luther heard someone tell his stripper date, "Look at the scars on that wetback, would ya?"

Luther glanced over at the skinny woman and she smiled at him. "You gonna do good," she said. "I can feel it, boo."

They fought off River Road, on some weed-choked industrial property between the levee and the Mississippi. The spectators made a limp ring around them, and because the Mexican was bigger and stronger but older and slower, Luther spent the first few minutes of the fight dancing—landing a jab here and there, but for the most part staying clear. The Mexican mainly threw heavy rights, pawing like a bear with his left as he tried to close the distance between them.

The Mexican had come alone but Luther had his uncle Melvin with him, an old cruiserweight who knew how to patch cuts and such. "Keep them hands loose," he hollered. The Mexican squared his shoulders and let fly with a straight kick. His work boot caught Luther low in the stomach, and Luther doubled over, then tried to turn his head away because he knew the big right would be coming. And the big right did come. It caught him on the side of the head and he felt an electric shiver run down the entire length of his body. His eyes clouded and he dropped to a knee. Uncle Melvin screamed, "Here he come," and Luther caught a blurred glimpse of the Mexican's boots shuffling closer. He shot out for a leg and took the man down. Luther was on top but didn't want to wrestle. He scrambled to his feet before the Mexican could grab solid hold of him. They were up again, circling. "Watch them kicks," Uncle Melvin yelled.

The Mexican was a bulldog. Luther danced and danced but still he came, pushing forward with his head down, absorbing punches as he waited for Luther to make another mistake. They drifted with the slope of the land as they fought, and when they reached the riverbank, the cheering crowd parted and let them splash on into the water. They were ankle deep in the dirty

Mississippi. Doyle ordered them to come back, but the fighters weren't listening.

Luther could tell that the Mexican was beginning to gas from punching air. The tired man continued to scratch with his left hand and at last Luther decided to throw the overhand right he'd been saving. He sank his foot in the soft river bottom and drove hard, swiveling his hips as he launched. The punch landed dead center and Luther felt the Mexican's nose break. But still he didn't drop. Blood poured from his shattered nose and collected in the water. The Mexican wiped his face with a wet hand and charged. Luther turned for high ground but the water and the mud robbed him. The Mexican caught him by the waist and they fell in a splashing heap. He had Luther dead to rights, was on top of him in the shallows forcing his head underwater. Uncle Melvin was yelling, "Get off, motherfucker, 'fore I shoot you," when Luther finally rolled free. He missed with a punch and again the Mexican grabbed him. They wrestled deeper and deeper into the river until the current began to pull at them both. The Mexican lost his footing, couldn't swim. He panicked and began to flail. Luther made a bid for his outstretched hand but it slipped away. The Mexican spun twice in the current and then disappeared beneath the surface. Luther went to the shore and a woman started crying. "Oh my God," she was saying. "Oh my God, oh my God, oh my God."

But nothing had ever come of it. Nothing. Doyle wrote down the names of everyone there that day, said it'd be a real mistake for them to ever go talking about this. And, far as Luther knew, the body was never even found—or at least not identified. It was like his uncle told him on the first of their three buses back to the projects: no body, no crime. Uncle Melvin shook his head. "You should have seen the blood in that water," he said. "I swear y'all looked like a couple of bleeding fish."

Luther told him to keep quiet, now and forever.

There was only a short silence before his uncle laughed. "Start calling you the Redfish!" he said.

And they did.

Shonda had the windows down. Luther woke early Sunday afternoon and could smell salt marsh mixed with the pines that grew in a thin stretch along the berm of the highway. Her battered Dodge Diplomat skipped across tidal streams as it crossed a series of small bridges that led to a larger one. Shonda punched his arm and told him that big river down there was the Pearl.

Luther wiped a seed of sleep from his eye and licked the scum from his teeth. He was still in his stiff work clothes, and his boots felt tight on his feet. "You really from out here?" he asked.

"You know it."

"Damn, girl," he said. "You country."

"Holler, Redfish."

Luther sighed. Shonda had moved into the St. Bernard Projects just a few weeks back, about the same time his grandmother had finally told him that he needed to go on and find a place of his own. They met at PJ's, had one drink before they wound up in her bed. In the morning Shonda said she'd feel a whole lot safer in St. B. with a big-ass man like him around. They'd lived like that ever since.

"Want me to drive?" he asked.

Shonda shook her head and sent the white beads in her hair clicking. "Naw," she drawled. "You done missed all the traffic."

"Sorry about that," said Luther.

"Yeah, I bet you real sorry," said Shonda. "But we about there now anyways."

The sky was big and blue and Luther breathed it in, ashamed to tell her that this was his first time ever out of the city as a free man. The tires hummed beneath them, and the Pearl River bridge descended, gave way to asphalt. Another several miles and Shonda turned off the highway.

Her mother lived down a gravel road, in a trailer set back in the pines. Luther saw that the windows had been boarded up, the raw yellow plywood spray-painted with the citations of Bible passages he didn't know: Genesis 9:11, Psalm 23:4. The Dodge stopped just ten yards from the trailer, and Luther stepped out and stretched. Shonda climbed the steps and waved him over. The door was unlocked and he followed her inside.

Luther's eyes were still adjusting to dim trailer when he registered the figure sitting in the corner with a shotgun. The man flicked his cigarette onto the dull blue carpet. "Woo-ee," he said.

Shonda screamed. "What you doing here?"

The man was staring at Luther. He had a bottle of Wild Irish Rose pinned between his knees. "Who's this motherfucker?" he slurred.

Shonda took a small step away from Luther. "Where's my mama, Freddie?"

"I put her on a bus," said the man. "Don't you worry about her."

"You did what?"

"I figured she'd come for her mama." Red-eyed Freddie smiled at Luther. "I know my wife."

"Wife?" said Luther.

Freddie leveled the shotgun at Luther's crotch, then took a pull from the bottle and licked his wet lips. "Looks like maybe you know her pretty well too."

"Wife?" said Luther again.

"I ain't scared of no big man," said Freddie. He tossed Shonda a roll of duct tape, ordered her to wrap Luther's ankles and wrists real good and tight.

They left him laid out on the linoleum floor of the kitchen. Freddie dragged Shonda outside, and she called them both a couple of punk cowards as the door slammed shut. After a while Luther heard Freddie's hidden car start up behind the trailer. He looked at the empty wallet resting next to his head, and a dark piece of his heart hoped that Freddie would take that lying woman down the road and shoot her.

On the kitchen table a digital clock marked the time in fluorescent green, but then went dark at midnight when the power failed. It was black inside the trailer now, and Luther counted out minutes to keep the time. Near as he could figure, it was another long hour before he was finally able to work his hands free. He pulled himself across the room, felt around through drawers and cabinets until he found a flashlight under the sink. He snapped it on and unraveled the tape binding his ankles, saw that his wrists were rubbed raw and bleeding. Standing, he went to the sink and tried the water. Dry. The trailer pulled from a well—the pump needed electric.

In the dead fridge Luther discovered a gallon of apple juice. He hooked his finger through a loop on the neck of the glass jug, balanced it in the crook of his arm as he drank. Just then the narrow trailer began to rock in the wind, and juice ran down his chin onto the front of his work shirt. Luther tried the phone but there was no dial tone. He opened the door and made his way down the steps.

Shonda's Diplomat sat crooked in the dusty hardpan, two of its tires slashed across the sidewalls. The trunk was open, and he could see that the garbage bags holding his clothes were missing. "Goddamn," he said. A light salty mist began to fall, and the wind in the pines made a sound like faraway applause. Luther walked back inside. He was hunting for spare batteries when he found Shonda's mother taped up in the bedroom closet.

They'd come for him in the first week of summer 1999. He was eating breakfast with his grandmother when he heard "Police! Search warrant!" a moment before the door was ripped off its hinges. A stun grenade bounced into the room and exploded in a flash-bang of blindness and confusion. Luther dropped to the floor as men in black washed over him. His grandmother was under the table and moaning. Tears dripped from Luther's cheeks as he tried to tell the cops where her pills were.

The old woman's wig was off, and her bald head shone like some blue-black melon. Luther took a step back, wincing at the sour smell of piss. "Damn," he said. "How long you been in here?"

She looked up at him, blinking. Luther knelt down beside her and brushed his fingers across the duct tape covering her mouth. "Don't be afraid," he told her. "I'm friends with Shonda."

Luther balanced the flashlight on his shoulder and shrugged, pinning it in place against his neck. He began to peel the thick tape from the woman's ankles and wrists. It came easily at first, the tape, but then he reached the final layers and in tender places her tissue-paper skin threatened to tear. "I'm so sorry, ma'am," he said. "So sorry."

Once her hands were free, he stepped aside and let the woman pull the tape from her face at whatever pace she could handle. She worked quicker than he would have and as the last of it came off Luther saw that her mouth was open wide, like Freddie had silenced her in the act of screaming.

"You okay?" he asked.

The woman spit a thread of green phlegm into the hem of her filthy nightgown. "What you think?"

Luther held out his hand but she pushed it away and rose with no help from him. It was not until he passed her the flashlight, put her in control, that he was able to convince her that he meant her no harm. He told her about Freddie running off with Shonda and all she did was shake her head. "Serves them both right," she said in a high, quick voice. "Them two deserve each other."

"I guess."

"You got a name?"

"Luther."

She gave a sharp nod. "I'm Betty," she said. The woman retreated into the bathroom with the flashlight, and Luther listened in the dark as she tried the shower and cursed. When she came back out she was naked.

Luther turned his head. "Whoa now, Miss Betty," he said.

Betty ignored him and pushed past with a towel slung over her bony shoulder. Luther heard the front door open and hurried after her. The rain was falling steady now. He stood on the concrete steps, searching. She had left the flashlight lying beside the door, and Luther took it into his hands, playing the beam through the pines until he found her.

She stood naked in a clearing—her head thrust back, her arms stretched out. Rain ran in sheets down her small wrinkled body. Luther could see that she was smiling, maybe even laughing. "You all right?" he hollered. Betty shook her head quickly from side to side but said nothing. "Come on," said Luther. "You gonna get hurt out there."

After he'd arrived at Angola, Luther began spending whatever free time he was allowed in the prison library. He found solace among those books, a place where he could escape the attention a giant receives in the yard. With nothing else to do he studied the law, learned how to challenge his murder sentence with motions and writs that he wrote out by hand and filed with the court of appeals. For a time the library meant hope—but that hope began to fade as, one by one, his pleadings were denied. After four years he was all out of legal theories.

It was at the onset of this dark period that Luther was called into the warden's office. His attorney from the trial was sitting there, the same fat man who had tried to hug him when the jury verdict was read. The warden shook Luther's hand and told him that he'd be free to go within the week. Congratulations, another big black man has confessed to your crime.

A *Times-Picayune* reporter had tracked him down after he was back in the city living with his grandmother. She asked Luther how it felt to be free, and he stared at her until she blushed and admitted that it was a stupid question. But her next one was no better: "Mr. Jackson, what was it like to be an innocent man in prison?" Luther ended the interview. He wasn't innocent, he felt like telling her. He just hadn't killed *that* man.

Betty sat down across from him in the living room and shined the flashlight into his eyes. She had dried herself off and put on a clean pink housecoat, big fuzzy slippers. This was an interrogation. "What you doing running around with a married woman?" she asked him.

All his practice lying—an entire lifetime, it seemed—and still Luther didn't know how to answer without putting the poor woman's daughter in a bad light. Finally he stopped trying. He told the story straight but simple. "I didn't ask for none of this," he added.

Betty appeared to soften. "You hungry?" she asked.

"Yes, ma'am."

"Stay there, then," she told him. "I'll be right back."

Betty went into the kitchen and returned carrying a cardboard box. Inside were a can of Sterno and a book of matches, a small pot, two bowls, and two spoons. For food, she had five small cans of Campbell's, all different flavors—that and a jug of water she had stashed somewhere.

Luther hadn't eaten since Quinn gave him half of his ham-and-cheese poboy the night before. He eyed the soup and Betty caught him staring. She told him to take his pick.

"You sure?"

"We'll share," she said. "Now choose."

He settled on vegetable beef and Betty passed him the can to open. She wiggled her fragile fingers. "Those flip tops," she said, "are murder on my old hands."

Luther pried open the lid and poured soup into the pot. Betty cut it with splashes of fresh water, then stirred the mixture with a few dainty stabs of her spoon. Luther lit one of the Sternos, and Betty killed the flashlight. They talked while Luther balanced the pot over the flame. He told her that, last he'd heard, the hurricane was still a category 5, would be making landfall sometime after sunrise.

Betty nodded. "Then we should get some sleep before morning," she said. "Big day tomorrow."

There was a flatness to her voice that Luther recognized from the projects, prison. The Sterno's flickering séance light illuminated her polished face and he was frightened by her expression, thought he saw something of that dead-eyed fatalism that'd been following him around his whole damn life.

Luther didn't sleep. He couldn't ever, not really. Instead he lay all night on the couch listening to the angry wind and Betty's peaceful snores echoing from the back bedroom. She had lent him an old silver wind-up watch that had belonged to her dead husband. It told Luther that it would be daylight soon, and sure enough, it wasn't long before the sun penetrated the thin gaps between the plywood boards covering the windows. Gray light filled the trailer and Luther sat up and put on his boots. Water was flowing beneath him; he could hear it. He walked across the living room and opened the door. "Fuck," he said.

The Pearl had overflowed its banks and flooded the woods surrounding the trailer. Pines blew like wheat in the wind; the clearing was a white-capped sea. The water lapped at the front steps, and Luther realized that it was still rising. He watched as a gust of wind sent a wave surging through the pine forest. Water slapped against the top step of the trailer and soaked his feet. He saw that Shonda's Dodge had been swept off in the night.

Luther heard Betty cough behind him. "Well," she said. "What you looking at?"

"Water," he said. "A whole lot of water."

Betty sidled up next to him to take a look. "Hmph," she said.

"We need to get on the roof."

"I'm not getting on any roof, Luther."

"We wait much longer we liable to get trapped in here."

"Maybe."

Luther shook his head and looked out the door. The water was skimming into the trailer now. There was a splashing off to his left and he saw a pair of jet-black feral hogs swimming hard, fighting their way to the high ground of the highway.

Betty pointed. "Pigs," she said. "Close the door."

"We close this door there won't be no opening it again." Luther took her by the wrist. "We gotta go," he said.

"I done told you I'm staying."

"We'll see."

The wind picked up even more and started snapping pines. A heavy branch crashed nearby and Luther flinched. Betty tried to close the door herself but he stopped her. "No," he said. "You gonna make a tomb out of this trailer."

Betty pinched him on his arm but retreated to the sofa. The water was past their ankles, and she kicked off her wet slippers. "All my things are getting ruined," she said.

Luther admitted that they were. "Still," he said. "Ain't nothing in here can't be replaced except me and you."

Betty took up the family Bible resting on her warped coffee table. "That's not true at all," she said. "Not one damn bit."

It was at that moment that Luther decided he would leave her, figured he'd be lucky just to make it through the storm on his own. "Stay here, then," he told her. "I'm gonna go check things out."

Betty pulled her bare feet up onto the sofa and refused to look at him. "Suit yourself," she said. "But you leave that watch right here with me."

Luther inched his way out of the trailer and down the sunken steps. The water ran past his waist and rain stung his face. He turned and put the worst of the weather at his back as he shuffled along with the current. In the distance he could see Shonda's lost car. The Dodge was wedged between two pines and holding steady against the current. A popping sound and he turned. The roof of the trailer was starting to buckle from the wind; an entire corner was peeled back like the lid from one of Betty's soup cans. Luther stood frozen as the hurricane punished him. He was halfway between the trailer and Shonda's car. The car. It had to be the car. And so he went for it. His boots were like bricks on his feet as he dogpaddled his way through the pines.

He was exhausted when he reached the trapped Dodge. The hood was slippery and he cut his hands trying to pull himself out of the water. He leaned back against the windshield and watched the rain blow sideways through the trees. A rabbit swam by and he thought of Betty, dead or dying. He could have brought her with him, forced her along. Luther wondered what that meant for his soul—not trying to save someone who didn't want saving. He saw his blood mixing with the floodwater and was reminded of that mythic fight that had made his name. Truth be told, he always took more than a little pride in being called the Redfish, coming out of that bloody water alive. Hell, he admitted, he was the Redfish. And that might just be what had kept him alive all these years.

Fall

Rabbit Man

MILAM RAISED MEAT rabbits, and what wasn't dead was dying. All save a few were bleeding from their nares. Hemorrhage. Hell. The old man sighed, then watched two more of his Hotots die as he waited for the federal inspector to drive over from Baton Rouge.

Something familiar. It clicked. The rabbit blood reminded him of that distant Sunday his carton-a-week wife collapsed at the altar of Holy Ghost, a crimson flower blooming on the handkerchief she'd pressed against her face. Milam shook his head to clear the image as he opened the door of the hutch that sheltered Gretta, heavy with kits. The big white doe still seemed healthy, and Milam gathered her into his arms.

It was early October but still hot as summer. A train rumbled by, rattling the tin shed and setting a distant crow to caw. The tracks ran just behind the chainlink fence that bordered the yard, and, with his free hand, Milam out of habit waved to the engineer before taking Gretta inside his home, away from the dying rabbits.

In the living room the grandfather clock announced nine A.M. Milam whispered, "Love you, Dottie," then placed Gretta on the kitchen floor. The clock had been a gift to his wife, a surprise for their fiftieth. When it chimed he told her he loved her. Even on the one-strike half-hours. Even in an empty house.

Gretta watched him pour cool tap water into an aluminum pie pan, then followed like a puppy as he walked to the bathroom. Milam knelt, set the pan down, and stroked her soft back while she drank. He made a nest of towels where she could bed down, and his pregnant girl was still drinking when he slipped quietly back into the hallway. He clicked the bathroom door shut behind him.

The inspector would be arriving soon. Milam went outside and settled onto his front step with a cinnamon roll. He lived maybe a mile off 190, in an ethnic ghetto of sorts. A Gaza Strip of Cajuns wedged between the Union Pacific line and the settlements of the Opelousas black majority. Two teenagers, shirtless in the heat, sauntered past his square prefab, all headphones and attitude as they laughed and traded rhymes about the crazy Rabbit Man. Milam glared after them.

The lady from the USDA introduced herself as Dr. Susan Wall. She handed Milam a business card, and he tucked it into the front pocket of his shirt. They walked out back together, and he watched as she gave his rabbitry a quick once-over. She hadn't been five minutes in the shed when she turned to him and asked if he would go ahead and kill the remaining ten Hotots for her.

Milam flinched. "The hell I will."

"It's plague, sir." The veterinarian removed a pair of latex gloves from her thin hands. "Calicivirus disease. No cure. Wiped out all the rabbits at the stock show up in Shreveport last weekend."

Milam grunted, and Dr. Wall gave him a sympathetic look. Suddenly there was tenderness in her blue eyes. She was very young, and it seemed impossible to him that she was a doctor of any sort. Maybe it was her hair, he thought, white blond and cut boy short.

"Did you have any rabbits at that show, Mr. Fourcade?"

"No." Milam drew a half-moon in the dirt with the toe of his filthy house slipper. "But I stopped by Friday afternoon," he admitted. "I wanted to see the rabbits. They had all kinds up there, you know?"

"Sure." Dr. Wall removed a trembling buck from his hutch. "And did you handle some of the stock?"

"I did."

"Then you went home and handled some of your own rabbits?"

Milam wiped his hands across his stiff khakis and nodded.

"And they began to get sick maybe five or six days later?"

"I guess, lady." He was tired of playing the student.

"I'm real sorry, sir, but there's no choice. We've been chasing this outbreak all over the state." Dr. Wall held the sick rabbit out to him, and Milam took a quick step back. "They're no danger to people," she assured him, reading his mind.

"You know that for certain?"

"I do."

He finally accepted the buck, one of his breeding stock. Clyde and Gretta. His original male, original female. Blood bubbled from Clyde's nose and fell in great drops onto the ground. Milam watched the blood mix with dust and become paste.

"If we don't get a handle on this soon," said Dr. Wall, "it could wipe out a lot more farmers like yourself."

Forty-odd years in the oil patch was the closest Milam had ever come to working the land, but he didn't correct her. Truth was, he liked being called a farmer. It made him feel part of something bigger. And that, he realized, was the same thing his wife used to say about church.

There are two easy, no-blood ways to kill a rabbit.

One: Hold the hind legs, its head pointing down. After a few seconds the rabbit will stop struggling and hang quietly. Then, with the edge of the palm of your free hand, or with a pipe or a stick, give a quick, chopping blow to the back of its neck.

Two: Some prefer dislocating the neck. Hold the hind legs with one hand, then place the thumb of your other hand just behind the ears, with your fingers grasping the throat. Pressing down on the thumb while quickly pulling the rabbit upward dislocates the neck.

Milam alternated between the two methods of execution, and, either way, the rabbits died swiftly and without much pain. He finished with five tiny kits that Dr. Wall had missed during her first pass through the shed. They were maybe a week old, still too small to clear the top of their jump box. Milam lifted the babies from the wooden box and killed them one at a time, placing each thin neck between his thumb and forefinger and then giving a slow, gentle squeeze.

His rabbitry destroyed, Milam walked with Dr. Wall to the front yard. He leaned against the side of her government-issue Ford and listened as she called back to her office for a cleanup crew. A cleanup crew. Like he's got an oil well back there that's just been capped. Milam was picturing spacemen in HAZMAT suits when Dr. Wall flipped her cell phone shut and turned to him.

"They want me to ask whether you've sold any rabbits since your trip to Shreveport."

Milam told her yes—but just one, to a pretty woman who wanted a bunny for her daughter's birthday party. He didn't sell too many rabbits as pets, at least not until Easter came around.

"Do you remember her name?"

He shook his head. "But she paid with a check—so she was local, I know that."

"Still have that check?"

"It's already cashed."

"I need you to come with me to your bank. Would you do that for me?"

Milam hesitated, then remembered the other farmers and agreed. He climbed into the passenger seat of the white Taurus, and Dr. Wall backed out the driveway, swinging wide to miss a broken-down Big Wheel some kid had left blocking the center of Raymond Street.

The teller at Teche Federal grinned at Milam's house slippers but was nice enough. She found his check in good order and printed him out a copy. In the top-right corner, superimposed over a picture of a magnolia blossom, was the information that Dr. Wall needed:

Mr. & Mrs. William LaFleur
15 Pintail Drive
Opelousas, LA 70570

Milam ran a cracked thumbnail over the broad loops of Mrs. LaFleur's signature. "Elizabeth. Her name was Elizabeth. I remember that now."

"Any idea where Pintail Drive is?" Dr. Wall asked him.

Milam shook his head and glanced over at the teller, aware that she had been eavesdropping. She blushed and he nodded his head, giving her permission to speak.

"It's over in Beau Canard," she said in a rush. "That new country club north of town."

Milam cut the girl off as she began to give them directions. "I know the place," he said. "I'll show her."

He headed for the door, and Dr. Wall fell in beside him. "You don't have to come, Mr. Fourcade."

Milam shrugged and Dr. Wall took his hand as they stepped

from the curb onto the parking lot, even opened his door for him. Sweet girl, he thought. He waited in the hot car as she walked around to the driver's side. She slid behind the steering wheel, and he asked if they should call ahead to Mrs. LaFleur.

"It would be better just to show up unannounced." Dr. Wall stretched her mouth into a thin smile. "People can be funny about their pets."

Milam remembered Gretta hidden away in his bathroom and nodded. He began directing Dr. Wall out of town, and when they passed the cemetery on Market Street he gave a slight nod toward the mausoleum—though not so obvious that Dr. Wall would notice. He and Dottie had bought three crypts: one for the twins, one apiece for themselves. All in a row like drawers in a filing cabinet, rabbit hutches in a shed.

Dr. Wall turned onto the highway, and Milam pulled himself away from the cemetery, away from memories of shoebox coffins and silk christening gowns. The lovebugs were swarming, maybe for the last time that year. He watched them collect on the windshield as Dr. Wall drove north to Beau Canard.

"Are you going to Maggie's birthday party?" The security guard was damn near his age, Milam decided, even looked a little familiar. A former classmate, perhaps. Dr. Wall smiled politely as she handed the old man an identification card of some sort.

"Feds, huh?" The guard pondered the ID, even flipped the card over to examine the back. "I think maybe I should call over there first."

"I would prefer if you didn't," said Dr. Wall.

The guard mulled that over. Behind him, a uniformed kid slouched in a folding chair and smirked at his stonewalled boss. "Well, they're probably all outside for the party, anyway," the guard said. He turned to his sullen teenage charge. "I'll send Officer Landry for you to follow," he added, saving face.

"That would be fine," said Dr. Wall.

Officer Landry, maybe eighteen and clearly outranked, sighed in response to his orders. With great effort he rose from his chair. He dropped his cigarette into a coffee can, then grabbed a set of keys from the pegboard. Milam felt a measure of sympathy for the kid. He knew a little bit about crap jobs.

The east–west streets of Beau Canard were named for ducks, the cross streets for geese, shore birds, that sort of thing. At the intersection of Specklebelly and Teal, Dr. Wall turned left and continued on to Pintail Drive, following Officer Landry's Corolla and its flashing yellow light.

Pintail Drive ended in a cul-de-sac, and balloons were tied to the mailbox of number 15. A line of parked cars stretched down the street and back again, but Officer Landry just parked behind the SUV in the driveway.

Dr. Wall pulled in behind him, then told Milam it probably would be best if he waited outside for now. That was fine by Milam. His nerve had faded in this neighborhood of the rich. Of golf-course dads and tennis-court moms. He watched from the passenger seat as Dr. Wall marched up the driveway. She rang the doorbell and was invited into the house by a little girl in a party hat.

Milam stepped outside to stretch his legs. He walked over to where Officer Landry was leaning against the side of his Toyota, smoking. "I'm Milam Fourcade," he said.

"Josh Landry." The kid was examining a fleck of tobacco he'd scraped off the tip of his tongue. He wiped his thumb clean on the front of his gray uniform before shaking Milam's hand. "You weren't related to Miss Dottie Fourcade, were you? The librarian over at the junior high?"

"I was her husband," said Milam.

"No kidding? I was real sorry to hear she passed." Officer Landry dropped his cigarette onto the driveway, scarring the concrete as he ground it out with the toe of his black Reebok. "A real nice lady," he added, almost to himself.

Milam nodded, watching as the kid fumbled in his shirt pocket for another smoke.

"What's this all about, anyway?"

"I sold Mrs. LaFleur a poisonous rabbit."

Officer Landry arched an eyebrow and considered him. "Yeah?"

"All my rabbits caught disease."

"I didn't even know y'all raised rabbits."

"It's just something I started doing after Dottie died."

Officer Landry spun the unlit Camel between his teeth. He started to speak but was interrupted by Dr. Wall exiting the house. She was holding a plastic Winn-Dixie bag, and from behind her, framed in the doorway, Elizabeth LaFleur glared out at them. Milam shuffled over to apologize, but Mrs. LaFleur turned away and shut the door. Not that he could blame her.

It was high noon and Africa hot. As Dr. Wall drove out of Beau Canard, Milam watched a black man in a riding lawn mower pass over a wet newspaper hidden in the grass. The *Daily World* exploded into confetti, and the yardman mouthed a curse as he dismounted to pick up the pieces.

Dr. Wall eased over a speed bump and told Milam what she had learned. How on the morning of little Maggie's birthday, Mrs. LaFleur had to explain to her daughter all about bunny heaven while Mr. LaFleur triple-wrapped Hoppy in plastic, embalming her until trash day in the garage chest freezer.

Milam winced at the story, sorry for little Maggie, sorry for bringing death to her house. He reckoned he should probably send Mrs. LaFleur a check when he got the chance. Maybe stop by with a healthy bunny on Easter. If he could make it past the guards. If he ever got back into the rabbit business. He smiled tight. That'd be a sight. The return of Hoppy from bunny heaven. And on Easter, no less. Milam decided against it. Probably be best for the girl to learn the big lesson now: things die, they stay dead.

The golf course was still littered with sticks and leaves from Rita, almost two weeks previous. Dr. Wall braked to let a pair of carts cross the road to the seventh hole, and Milam watched as they wound down the clamshell path, following a chemical green fairway that ran like spilled paint through second-growth hardwoods. Hoppy defrosted in the trunk as Milam imagined the wild rabbits, the cottontails and the swampers, that would appear at dusk to feed along the course edges.

The cleanup crew was waiting for them in the backyard, and they had the dead Hotots piled just a few feet from the bathtub grotto. A blood sacrifice to Mary at the place where Milam lit Sunday candles for Dottie and the twins. A thin man with a clipboard approached Dr. Wall, and Milam listened as they discussed complicated plans for disinfection, quarantine, disposal.

Clipboard Man was all business, and he reminded Milam of that long-ago pediatrician at the General. The doctor who sat Milam down and told him about bacteria in the spinal fluid. Meningitis. Dottie fainted and that doctor had kept on talking, telling Milam how maybe, if he had brought the babies in sooner, they might have stood a chance.

The sun bore down on the yard, and flies were collecting on the dead. Milam excused himself to the house for a glass of water, and Dr. Wall patted him on the shoulder. She thanked him for all his help, for being so understanding. Go inside where it's cool, she told him. Get some rest. We'll be out here awhile.

Milam had left red beans to soak overnight on the stovetop. He drained them in the sink and decided he'd better go ahead and move Gretta. One of the USDA crew might ask to use his bathroom, and of course that wouldn't do.

He'd been putting it off, checking on Gretta. Didn't want to open that door and see his original doe blowing red and dying. Milam took a deep breath and eased into the bathroom slowly, damn near cried in relief when he saw fresh-faced Gretta cat-curled in her nest of towels. Her nostrils twitched when she smelled him, and then she hopped right over.

Gretta followed him as he moved her water and her towels into the laundry room next to the kitchen. She made a lazy attempt to escape, but he slid the flimsy door shut. The bi-fold door closed the same way a book opened, and when Milam saw Gretta's whiskers poking out from between the cheap wooden slats he was happy for the first time that day.

A black woman who lived on the other side of Raymond cut up the Cajun holy trinity for him, stopping by every few weeks with a Cool Whip tub of onions, bell peppers, and celery she'd diced. Charity for the Rabbit Man to make her right with the Lord. Fine by him. Milam heated a measure of bacon grease in his Dutch oven, then sautéed two great handfuls of the trinity until the vegetables were crisp-tender, the onions clear. He smelled garlic frying. Lagniappe. Why, thank you, Miss Cora. He added a few slices of pickled pork from Savoie's and a link of the rabbit sausage his butcher made for him special, dusting it all with Tony's before he finally dropped in the tender beans and some clean water, a couple of bay leaves. He set the mix to simmer.

Milam made sweet wine from the muscadine and black-berry that grew in wild tangles along the railroad tracks behind the house. A jug of it sat atop the icebox, corked and waiting, and he went for it now. Milam poured four fingers into a coffee mug and settled down at the kitchen table. The creak of hinges came from his left and, turning, he saw that Gretta had forced her way out of the laundry room, pushing against the spine of the door until it collapsed in like a Bible closing. His pregnant doe presented herself in the doorway. "Sneaky girl," said Milam.

Gretta hop-slid across the linoleum, and Milam placed her on his lap. He offered a handful of trinity, and she fed from his palm as he took a long, slow pull from his mug. A window looked out onto the backyard from the kitchen, and he remembered too late what he'd been forgetting. His hand trembled and wine spilled from his lips, cutting a ruby line down the front of his white shirt. Dr. Wall's pretty face was framed in the window, her ice blue eyes watching him watching her.

The grandfather clock struck noon. Milam told his wife he loved her as he grabbed hold of Gretta's hind legs.

The Rapture

BIZ FOLSOM, that's my new floor boss. You should see the son of a bitch: pressed Wranglers, George Strait Resistol—thinks he's a cowboy. He cradles his pie plate of a belt buckle, daring me to push him. "Either pull yourself together," he says, "or get your sweet ass on home."

He's sore at me for refusing a lap dance to some drunk. "I don't know how y'all did it in New Orleans," he says, "but you don't get to choose your customers here." Fuck this. I don't say nothing, just grab my bag and walk out the door dressed like a goddamn schoolgirl. I didn't make it through the storm to put up with his small-town bullshit.

Outside, a giant Pentecostal screams at deer hunters from the shoulder of the highway. He looks close to seven feet tall but is built like a rake. He calls me a whore. "You're gonna burn in hell," he says.

My ride home is inside swinging on a pole, so I holler right back at the skinny Bible beater. "Give me a lift," I tell him. "Be a good Christian." A logging truck rumbles by and the headlights play across his red face. He looks scared to death as I prepare to jump the ditch in my tiny plaid skirt.

The man's station wagon smells like insect repellent. We pull out onto the highway and his courage returns. "You dance for the Devil," he preaches. "The Enemy has made you his servant."

"Take a left here," I say, pointing at my turnoff.

It's a clear, cool evening, and deer are moving with the full moon, night-feeding in the soybean fields. A doe and two yearlings skitter across the gravel road, eyes phosphorescent. We brake, then roll on.

I'm back living with my mama in the same clapboard where I grew up. The freak preacher pulls in front of the house and kills the engine. "Will you pray with me?" he asks.

I figure that's the least I can do, seeing as how he gave me a ride and all. I take his big hand and listen to him ramble. The prayer drags on and on until finally I realize that he's stalling, doesn't really want to let me loose. I think that's pretty funny so I inch my hand closer to his thigh. My little finger brushes the hard-on pressing against his thin black slacks and his palm goes slippery with sweat. "Sister," he asks, his voice raspy, "is there anything at all that you would like to pray for?"

"I'll finish you off for fifty bucks," I tell him. "Amen."

He gives a quick gasp when I say that, then pushes my hand off like it's on fire. "Get away from me," he whispers.

I've never turned a trick in my life and don't plan on starting outside my mama's house with this clown. "Relax," I say. "I was only joking."

"Get away from me now," he repeats. "Please don't make me ask you again."

I take my time but do as he says. Coyotes are yipping in the distance and I sit on the porch to have a smoke and listen. I keep waiting for him to crank up his station wagon but the creepy fucker never does. The moonlight's reflecting off his windshield and I wonder what he's doing. He can see me but I can't see him, and since there was a time when I believed what he believes, I wonder whether it's finally happened. I wonder if he's gone and disappeared on me. Is it possible that the Tribulation has just now begun?

The High Place I Go

MY HUSBAND SCREWS AROUND. Not much and not often, but I know that Andy tries whenever he gets the chance. I know it, and he knows that I know it. I press him, and he says that if I want to split up he'll understand. That's him trying to pin it all on me. Trying to make it so he can tell our two boys that Mama was the one who left, that he'd hoped to make things work. He says to me that he loves me and that I'm still his best friend—that we'll always be best friends—but that maybe we just started out too young, had too much play left in us when we tied the knot. I've got a clock in my head that reads four years and four months. That's how long until our youngest turns eighteen and I can call a lawyer. Yessir. Four years, four months.

I wake up most days, all I see is red. Well, crimson. An Alabama Crimson Tide. Andy painted the walls of our bedroom cranberry after the coach was fired in 2000, even bought a secondhand RV for tailgating, celebrating that new beginning. He was making better money then, foreman money. That was before his drinking got him busted back to the line. He's lucky he wasn't fired himself, really.

Alabama plays Mississippi State at two thirty this afternoon. Andy and our boys left last night, rode over to Starkville in his brother's new RV. That Fleetwood puts our old Winnebago to shame, and I can't imagine that she'll be making too many more trips.

So here I am again, all by myself. Not that I'm complaining. I worked an eleven–seven at the VA last night, so burning a pig in some dusty parking lot—not exactly my idea of Saturday fun. Andy can keep all that for himself.

I slide over to the cool side of the bed and close my eyes, block out the 'Bama red and try to catch just a few more hours of sleep. In good time I'll pack a bag and leave the house, maybe drive down the road for a couple of hamburger sandwiches before I pick up Ryan and we set out for Rock City. I'm sixteen again, alone in my bedroom and in love with a boy.

Life happens in hospitals. That's one thing I've always liked about being a nurse. Babies arriving in one room, folks dying in another. There's no emergency department in the VA, but I still see plenty—and besides, I cut my teeth as a traveling nurse, so I've already experienced more than my fill of ER excitement. Back then they'd farm me out to hospitals with a shortage, or I'd play scab if nurses were striking somewhere. The money was good, and this girl from the hills of Tennessee got to see America, so to speak.

Andy calls those my whore days, half kidding, I guess. That started our first night together. He wasn't a minute inside me before he asked that I tell him about all the doctors I'd fucked. Said it just like that—drunken dirty talk—but I was game. He was on top of me in the motel room, and I was telling him, whispering in his ear about the Apache doctor and the Flagstaff supply closet; this famous neurosurgeon who flew me and another nurse out to the Hamptons for a week, put us up in a condo where we slept three across the bed every night. Damn, those stories would get Andy hot—still do when I'm willing to play that ace. I can see us one day, grandparents, Andy asking me to tell him about my whore days. I think about that sometimes and laugh. Christ, that there's reason enough not to stick around forever.

We met back when I was starting out as a nurse. I was just a girl—twenty-two, twenty-three—and pretty, real pretty. I would work my shift and change clothes at the hospital, hit the bar across the street. And, trust me, every hospital had a bar across the street. Places with goofy names like Scrubs and Stitches, Code Blues. I know, right?

Agency nurses were popular because we were temporary, wouldn't be stopping by Timmy's soccer game to see what the wife looked like. It was all about fun for us—but a month in a Howard Johnson will drive a girl crazy lonely. So crazy she'll find herself being double-teamed by EMTs in the back of an off-duty ambulance. So crazy she'll wake up and share a saline drip with the bastards just to kill the hangover. High times.

So this was how I met my husband: I was sitting at the bar in a place called Triage, just a stone's throw from Ochsner in New Orleans. It was eight A.M.—happy hour for the night shift—and I was drinking Cuba libres with this fighter-pilot ER doc when Andy walked up in his hardhat, said, Thanks for saving my seat, mister, your wife's looking for you out in the parking lot. The doctor wasn't buying it, but I could read his mind. *This mountain-trash jackleg nurse isn't worth the ass-whipping.* That was exactly what he was thinking when he shuffled away. I was pissed but not very. The kid was real cute, and he was also my age. He might not have been a doctor, but he didn't look to be married neither.

Andy was an Alabama boy, in town to work a turnaround at one of the Norco refineries upriver. We drank till noon at Triage, then he followed me in his pickup to my motel near the airport. We went at it so hard the maids were giggling outside our door, slept for a few hours, and then did it again. That night we both left for our shifts, and the next morning he was sitting on the hood of my rental car waiting for me to get off work. For a week we lived almost like a couple. Almost. The Ochsner strike ended about the same time Andy's refinery got back on-stream. We exchanged phone numbers and went our separate ways.

Two months later I was working a crowded ER in Orlando when Andy strolled in to surprise me. I told him that was the most romantic thing anyone had ever done for me—and, I'm really glad you came because I'm pretty sure I'm pregnant.

"Then I said unto them, 'What is the high place whereunto you go?' And the name thereof is called Bamah unto this day." Ezekiel 20:29. That's the gem Andy snuck into his vows at our wedding ceremony. Roll Tide, amen. You know my Tennessee family just loved that.

We married in Chattanooga, then moved to Tuscaloosa. Andy took a factory job, and I had Irish twins, two boys only ten months apart. Since I wasn't looking to field a team myself, I went ahead and had my tubes tied.

They're typical teenagers now, Bryant and Paul, don't ever want much to do with their mama. Every now and then I think that I should have held off on getting fixed, that if I'd tried for a girl everything might have turned out different, at least in some slight way.

The Winnebago sleeps like a hibernating bear in the carport next to the house. I drop my wedding ring in with the ashtray coins and back her down the driveway too fast, just miss clipping our mailbox before I straighten out and roll on.

I called ahead to the lunch counter at the Texaco, so the sweet black girl has my order sacked and ready when I pull up. The game's playing on the TV behind her, and I can see that Mississippi State's just kicking off. The girl catches me looking. "Roll Tide, Miss Karen," she says.

"Roll Tide," I say.

"You look real pretty."

I'm wearing tight jeans and a thin white peasant blouse that sits low on my shoulders. It feels nice to be noticed. "Thank you," I tell her.

"You going on a trip?"

"Maybe. Wanna come?"

The counter girl smiles a big toothy smile, and I wander to the back for two cold drinks. On the way I pass a rack of magazines and see a cheap one called *Husband & Wife.* Tim McGraw and Faith Hill are on the glossy cover, her in a tiny dress and him in his black hat. On our tenth anniversary, Andy took me to see them both in concert. They closed with a duet, and when they were finished Andy laughed and said, Boy, that Faith sure is something. I punched him in the arm and said that Tim's not too bad himself. I guess that gave Andy an idea. "Hey," he said. "You ever get a chance to roll with McGraw, you go on and take it."

"Oh yeah?"

"Yeah," he said. "I'll give you a free pass."

A free pass. That was before Andy had begun to stray, and so I played along, gave him Faith for our anniversary. It was a joke at the time, but I realize now that it's dangerous for a couple to start playing games like that. I swear, I think he was cheating before the month was out.

I linger by the coolers and try to remember whether it's Coca-Cola or Mountain Dew that Ryan likes better. I don't want to get this wrong, am hoping every little detail will be spot-on and perfect. I go with Mountain Dew, then pull three hundred bucks out of the cash machine. There's a dirty window off to my left. I look out and see the Winnebago at the pump, still steady drinking gas.

Lance Corporal Ryan Jordan began his stint in the VA about four months ago. Tuscaloosa by way of Germany by way of Baghdad. Before all that: Alpine, Alabama—a flyspeck hill town east of here. Poor Ryan's been stuck in a wheelchair for close to a year, will be for life, barring some miracle not even on the horizon. I've got fifteen years on him, could even be his mother, as they say—or would say, if they knew how I feel about him.

I work the inpatient rehab floor, one nurse monitoring a handful of spinals—young men being taught how to live the rest of their lives broken. Ryan's first night I rounded on his room, saw him quivering in his sleep like some dreaming dog, saw that he had sweat clear through his hospital gown.

Nightmare patrol, that's a lot of what I do for these boys.

I placed a wet cloth on his forehead, and he woke up shivering, staring at me with these blue eyes that were like swimming pools in his pretty face. I did a little double take. He looked just like Andy at that age. A dead ringer, I swear. My mouth went dry, and there was a taste like metal. I mopped his brow with that washcloth, and we just kept on staring at each other. He told me later that he recognized something in me as well, that I reminded him of an actress whose name he could never remember.

"Can you lift yourself up?" I'd asked him. "Can you lift yourself up if I help you?"

Ryan nodded. "You ready?"

"I'm ready."

He latched his hands on to the side rails and struggled to pull himself into a sit.

"Great," I said. "Now stick out your arms." He did as I asked, and I peeled the filthy gown from his body—then I spread a clean towel across the bed and told him to lie back down. "Thank you," I said. "Perfect."

That's really a CNA's responsibility, giving a sponge bath. But, again, it was Ryan's first night on the floor, and I didn't want him thinking that I couldn't be bothered. I filled a small tub with warm, soapy water and did his arms, then his legs, was moving across his stomach when I saw that he had an erection. That's common enough with quads and paras—and I don't think Ryan even realized it because he was still just watching me. I was cleaning his privates when he finally saw what was going on down there. He covered himself with his hands and gave me this horrified, humiliated look. And then he started to cry, apologizing, calling me ma'am.

"It's fine," I told him. "Really." I pushed his hands away and finished cleaning his front. "Now let's roll you on over."

His legs were still pretty well built, and his body was more or less perfect in proportion—but my eyes welled up when I saw his back, the angry red scars laid out like the lashes of a thick whip. He kept crying just a little as I washed down those scars and so, again, I told him that it was okay, don't you worry, baby.

And then I proved it to him shift after shift, washing him clean after every last bad dream.

I realize now that I was teasing him, that I liked the way it felt to have somebody want me again. But then one night I let him kiss me, and the score got a lot less lopsided in that game we were playing. I have an older sister I trust and tell everything. She lives back home in Tennessee with her perfect husband and her perfect kids. That next morning they stopped by on their way down to Gulf Shores. They spent the night, and I called in sick. While everyone slept, us sisters went on the back porch together and drank a bottle of wine. Charlotte's a real good listener, and she let me get it all off my chest about first base with Ryan. I told her that she probably couldn't understand how I could go and fall for a crippled boy. God bless Charlotte. She said, No, I get it fine. He digs you for you, and so you dig him for him. Just be careful, Karen. You know it has to stop right there.

But of course it didn't. Near the last of August, Ryan finished up with his PT, and they released him back into the wild. By then we'd been fooling around for a month, but I told myself that would have to be the end of it. My first shift without him, the remnants of Katrina dumped three inches of rain on Tuscaloosa County. The power went out, and the generators kicked on. I spent the night wandering those bright empty halls feeling miserable with worry. At last it got to where I couldn't take it. I went poking around in Records and found Ryan's phone number, the address of his apartment. I called him, and he said that he was doing just fine—but please please please come and see me sometime. I repeated what I'd told him the night before his discharge, my speech about how this thing between us was impossible. "Fine," he said to me. "Fine."

After that, a couple of times a week I'd ease by his place, sit in my car, and stare at the wheelchair ramp that led to his front door. I kept up my stalking through September but never once saw him. Then one day I peeked in his window, and he caught me watching. "Come on inside," he hollered. "Door's open." He didn't ask me to explain myself. He just took me and stripped me, put his head between my legs until it happened just like they write on this state's rocket-pop license tags. The stars fell on Alabama, and I was finally in love again.

It's November now, and I never let more than a few days go by without sneaking over to see him. He's got a drawer full of mail-order toys that he likes to use on me; seems like every visit it's something new and different.

At the very top of Lookout Mountain sits Rock City, a collection of big boulders arranged by God in such a way as to create a fairy-tale village of paths and lanes. It's like a little half-assed piece of Disney World in the hills, sort of tacky and beautiful all at the same time. My parents went there, and my parents' parents went there. You go for the views—that, and to look at funny rocks.

There's a bullshit legend that my family passes off as gospel. A story about Indian lovers who ran off together—our idea of romance. They came from feuding tribes, this couple. A Chickasaw boy and a Cherokee girl. The brave was captured by Cherokees and thrown to his death off Lookout Mountain, tossed from the same spot where they now say it's possible to see seven states on a clear day. They call that spot Lover's Leap—call it Lover's Leap because the Cherokee maiden jumped right on after her man.

When I was a girl it was my dream to be married at Lover's Leap, to exchange vows there on a pretty mountain morning. I'd wear a simple white dress and weave wildflowers into my hair. I'd told that to Andy, and he'd laughed, said that was just way too hippie for him.

Ryan lives on the first floor of this trashy apartment complex stuck between railroad tracks and the highway. It's a black neighborhood, really, what my hillbilly daddy would have called Jacundaville. I give the door a knock, and Ryan hollers me in like he's been expecting company.

He's shirtless in his wheelchair. The apartment is dark like a tomb, and a Marlboro haze hangs under the low ceiling. I set the food down on his shaky coffee table, then move across the room and give him a quick tongue kiss. His mouth tastes like charcoal. He starts to pull my blouse down, but I slap at his hands. "I brought you a hamburger," I say. "Thought you might be watching the game."

"Thanks." Ryan nods at the flickering television. "We just kicked a field goal."

"Great," I say, though I don't really care. "You're looking good."

That's only half true. He's broad across the chest and arms, but his legs are getting more and more thin. I can see that even through his jeans. He smiles and crushes his cigarette into the plastic ashtray balanced on his dead lap. "Clean living," he says.

I fetch napkins from the kitchen and notice dirty dishes, some broken glass. After we eat, I get to work. I clean the kitchen and the bathroom, pull up the blinds, open the door so as to let some of that beautiful fall weather inside. I know it embarrasses him, but I can't help myself. The mother in me, I guess.

Cleaning doesn't take too long, not for this tiny one-bed, one-bath. I hand Ryan a white T-shirt and his worn field jacket, talk him into having his next cigarette outside. He says okay, and that makes me glad. I'm hoping that maybe he'll get into the habit of taking fresh air when I'm not around.

Children have emptied out into the parking lot for a half-time recess. I roll Ryan over to the side, right where the asphalt drops off into a kudzu-choked washout. He smokes his cigarette, and we watch a group of black boys play a game—this game where one tosses a football up real high for the rest, then they fight and claw for the catch. Near as I can figure, three catches and you get to throw. It's a poor kids' game.

"So I have an idea, Ryan."

"Yeah?"

I nod over at the Winnebago, and for the first time he connects it to me. "That's us," I say.

"What are you talking about?"

"We're taking a trip."

"Where?"

"It's a surprise."

"What kind of surprise?"

"The kind you don't talk about." I pat him on his knee, like that's something he can feel. "Well?"

A boy hollers over at us. "Heads up," he says, but I turn too late. Ryan flinches as the football lands hard on the asphalt next to him; it skips past his wheelchair so low and fast that even I'm thinking grenade.

"Fucking niggers," Ryan whispers, real poisonous and mean. He's shaking a little, glaring at the spot where the football has disappeared into the kudzu. Finally those familiar blue eyes dart back my way, and he shrugs. "What else am I gonna do, Karen?"

It was his birthday; I knew that from his chart. Big twenty-one. I had spent all day making a red velvet cake, and I'd surprised him with it in his hospital room just before midnight. We'd washed down two great pieces with cold milk from the cafeteria, and later, Ryan got to staring at what was left of that cake and went serious. He asked me what kind of family he must have that doesn't even visit him on his birthday. I didn't know what to say, and he wouldn't stop concentrating on that cut cake, the red velvet looking like a bleeding wound. I held his hand and told him that time would make things work, though I've always believed that the opposite is probably true. That was when he started petting my wrist, real light at first, but I didn't move away and so I guess I let it become more serious. He tugged me closer and started kissing me like I hadn't been kissed in a decade. Damn, you have no idea how much I wanted to climb into that hospital bed with him, even just to hold him and watch infomercials for an hour. But I couldn't. Somewhere there was a line that I wasn't willing to cross, at least not right then, and so I pulled away.

The next shift Ryan gave me a single red rose from Lord knows where. The shift after that it was a sweet little poem. That boy chopped me down like a tall, tall tree, took me out section by section, until one night I quit fighting and fell into his bed.

It only takes a few minutes for Ryan and me to stuff his clothes and medical stuff into a couple of paper shopping bags. I see him throw in a battery-powered rubber something that looks like a baby's arm, and my stomach gives a quick roller-coaster bounce. The whole time Ryan's steady asking me where we're going, but I won't let on. "The excitement," I tell him, "is in the wondering."

We go outside, and I open the door on the side of the RV. Silver steps drop down, then Ryan sheds his jacket and rolls closer. His wheels hit up against the Winnebago, and he leans forward, grabs hold of the rail that runs alongside the magic stairway. I hurry over to help him, but he waves me away. "No," he says. "I can do this."

I take a step back and give him his space. Both his hands are still gripping the rail. He pulls himself out of the chair, and his body sort of falls and spins all at once. He's lying sideways on those dirty stairs, and so again I rush to him. "Come on and let me help you," I tell him.

"Stop it," he says.

So I do nothing. Ryan slides himself up into the RV, then elbow-crawls like a soldier all the way to the front—me following right behind in case he decides that he needs me after all. He situates himself in the shotgun captain chair, and I see that his T-shirt is all stretched out and dirty now. He's breathing heavy from the effort, and there's sweat collecting along the scar on the back of his pale neck. "See?" he says.

I duck back outside and collect his things. The wheelchair is sitting there empty and I fold it up flat. The sun is setting when I ease onto I-59, and finally I let Ryan know where it is that we're headed. He rolls his eyes when I tell him that we're going to see Rock City.

"You've been there?" I ask.

"Naw."

"How's that possible? Everybody's been there."

"Not my family," he says. "We didn't go places."

We stop for dinner north of Fort Payne, just a few miles after crossing the Georgia line. Andy rings my cell phone just as I'm pulling into the parking lot of a bar, this sprawled-out roadhouse claiming to serve food. I step outside to take the call, leave Ryan sitting there in the captain chair while I talk to my husband.

I already know from the radio that Alabama won—stayed undefeated—and Andy sounds drunk as the night we met Snake Stabler in the Flora-Bama. "Where you at?" he asks me. "I done tried the house twice already."

I tell him that I'm out running a few errands, and he doesn't press.

"Well, I'm just checking in," says Andy. "We'll be heading back tomorrow afternoon."

"Take your time. No rush."

I hear some laughter in the background and imagine a party that's probably not so different from the one Andy and the boys are really at. In my head I see women who are still only girls sitting two to an ice chest and teasing my shy sons. They have pretty brown legs and crimson ribbons in their hair. I picture them sipping big plastic cups of gin and tonic poured over lots and lots of crushed ice and cut lime. Good luck to you girls. Enjoy yourselves now. I mean it. I really, really do. We say our half-assed I-love-yous, and then I shut off the phone.

What's a plain old Saturday evening to you and me is Steak Night to the folks at the Carousel Bar and Grill. A teenage wait-ress shows us to our table, just a couple of steps from this little circular stage that's revolving three-sixty, spinning round so slow that I barely notice it moving. No band's in sight—thank God—but there's a card table set up on the stage. Four men are playing what looks to be poker, that all-in hold'em you see on TV. They sit still as statues, their faces hidden behind wrap-around sunglasses and these veils of camouflage mesh.

I glance over at Ryan. "What the hell?"

"Facemasks," he says. "For turkey hunting."

"But why?"

"To keep from giving away their tells."

"It's okay for them to be gambling in here?"

Ryan shrugs and we order drinks, sign on for two specials, done medium. In a few minutes our waitress returns with a cold bottle of low-carb beer for me, a straight glass of Abso-lut for Ryan. He likes beer plenty, but it's a hassle for him, as fluids lead to pissing—call for things that he doesn't want to mess with here tonight, things like catheters and leg bags. He sips his vodka, and I sip my beer. Waiting for our food, watching those slow-spinning men play illegal cards above us, I can't help thinking about how much they look like wraiths. Absolute fucking wraiths.

I turn my attention back to Ryan and see that he has torn a cardboard coaster into a dozen small pieces. He told me once how it happened. I wonder sometimes when I'm driving what that must be like, to be rolling down the road and have your whole world explode in a flash of red.

After six or seven rounds I close out, and a sleeveless bouncer gives us permission to camp in the parking lot overnight. If it was a struggle getting Ryan up into the RV before, it's high comedy now. This time he even lets me help him, but, even still, we're not getting anywhere fast. Thank God a cowboy is passing by. He's stumbling a little himself, but between the three of us we're able to move Ryan into the tiny closet of a bathroom so that he can do his business before bed. The cowboy turns out to be a vet, a Marine like Ryan. Always faithful, those Marines. They exchange slurred *semper fis*, then he leaves us for that haunted card game.

Ryan's slumped on the toilet with his clothes on, and I go fetch his things so that he can empty himself out for the night. I come back carrying a big Ziploc full of catheters and latex gloves, lubes and suppositories. Even though I know that he'll refuse, I ask if he needs my help at all. "I'm a nurse," I tell him. "Remember?" Ryan shakes his head, then pushes the door shut.

He's in there for almost an hour. Twice I check on him, and both times he says, Hold on, I'll be out in a bit. I go outside and look at the stars, come back and fiddle with the radio. I'm listening to light country when at last the bathroom door opens and Ryan comes crawling out. I clear everything out of his way and wait for him on the bed in the cabin. When he climbs up there with me I realize that he's still a whole lot drunker than I am. He's in a dark, vodka place—and though I think maybe I want to fool around, he's not really responding, just wants to sleep. He starts snoring low, and I pull off his shoes, unbuckle his belt, and take down his pants. It's freezing in the RV, and of course the heater's broken. I gather up all the bedding that I can find, pile blankets and pillows on top of him, and slide naked into our nest.

I wake early in the half-light of dawn, Ryan twitching beside me. I think maybe he's having one of his nightmares until my thigh bumps up against his hard-on. I study his face, see that his mouth is set in a tight smile and decide that this is no nightmare. Ryan's making love to somebody in this dream. We've tried plenty but have never been able to do that together. Not once. I lie there watching, and for a while that's enough. I'm happy just to see him happy. But then something begins to stir, and, looking at him, I can't bear to be on the sidelines anymore.

Moving real quiet, careful not to wake him, I straddle those thin hips, slip that phantom erection inside of me, and slide across him in slow steady waves, waves that break and recede without ever touching that healthy part of him that might feel me and end this good dream he's having, this good dream we're both having. I bite the back of my hand to keep from moaning but don't quite come before the shame hits and I'm brought to my senses. I roll off him and start to cry. Somehow this of all things is what wakes the boy up. "What's wrong?" he asks. "Are you all right?"

"I'm fine," I tell him. "Were you dreaming?"

"What?"

"Before you woke up," I say. "Were you dreaming?"

"I don't think so."

"Really?"

"Really."

I like old movies, pictures like *Casablanca* and whatnot. I laugh and try to be funny. "Of all the hospitals in all the towns in all the world," I say.

It's eight o'clock in the morning when we pull into the RV lot at Rock City Gardens. Retiree gypsies are up and making breakfast on their Colemans. An old couple stands studying a big map they have spread out across a picnic table; mugs of coffee are steaming in their hands. They look up as we rumble past and wave happily. I wave back, then holler to Ryan, tell him that we're finally here. He's in the bathroom again, has been since we left the Carousel an hour ago. He yells something to me that I can't understand.

I park the Winnebago at a far, empty corner of the lot where no one will bother us. The ticket office opens in a half-hour, and I'm ready to go. This morning while Ryan slept I took a shower, changed into clean underwear and clean clothes. I'm wearing corduroys and a pretty pink fleece, comfortable shoes for walking. I go outside. It's sweet-aired and chilly. I set Ryan's wheelchair up at the bottom of the steps, then duck back into the RV to check on him. I figure we've got two hours before we have to leave if I want to beat Andy and the boys home from Starkville. I'm not sure I even care about that anymore, but, still, time's a-wasting.

Inside, the door to the bathroom opens, and I see Ryan sitting there wet-haired and naked. "Can you get me some clothes?" he asks.

"Of course, baby, of course." I go into the cabin and return with a flannel button-down and a pair of socks, fresh boxers and his Levi's. Ryan lays himself down on the floor, and we get him dressed without too much effort. He puts on his field jacket, and I tie his shoes, pull a knit watch cap over his head so that his ears won't get cold. "All set?" I ask.

"All set."

Ryan moves himself down the stairs feet first, shimmying his ass carefully from step to step like a slow-falling Slinky toy. When he reaches the bottom, I bring over the wheelchair and help him onboard. I look over and see that a dozen retirees are staring at us. I can hear them without hearing them. Bless his heart, they're saying. That poor young man.

I lock up the Winnebago, and we get moving. I ask Ryan if it would be okay if I push him, and he says sure, go ahead. The asphalt parking lot is as level as a board, and we roll easily along.

I can already see the stone buildings that mark the entrance. Out front a big-eared velvet gnome is shaking hands with a child. He's wearing curled red slippers and something like a Santa hat. Ryan points at him. "What the hell is that?"

"That's the mascot," I tell him. "Rocko, Rocky, I can't remember which."

"Jesus," says Ryan. "His nose looks like a dick."

The mascot comes wobbling toward us, but I wave him away.

Rock City Gardens is only partially handicapped accessible. That's what the cute girl tells us at the ticket counter. Goddamn it to hell. *Don't you cry, Karen. Don't you fucking cry.* We're shuffled off to the side and promised the escorted VIP tour, round-trip distance just one half mile. Ryan must see that I'm upset. "It's okay," he says. "We'll make the best of it."

And so we go. We follow the Georgia Peach up an employee

trail, and along the way we pass off-duty Rockys and chain-smoking taffy vendors. We're missing out on everything that I remember about this place—sights like the Deer Park and Mushroom Rock, Goblin's Underpass and the Swing-A-Long Bridge. "But don't y'all worry," our guide tells us. She pulls a videotape from her backpack and hands it to Ryan. "Our VIPs are given the *Rock City Adventure* video of the entire gardens. You'll just love it." Ryan says great, but I stay quiet. The girl keeps talking, says, "I like to think of this place as the Good Lord's rock garden." She tells us how it's a shame that we just missed out on Rocktoberfest—and then there's the Christmas lights, we're two weeks early for those.

Finally we reach the end of our trail, and I push Ryan's wheelchair to the overlook at Lover's Leap. So now here we are—me sitting on his lap, him holding the adventure video. Behind us the banners of the Seven States Flag Court pop and crack in the wind. I have to lean close for Ryan to hear me. I pull his head to my chest, peel up his watch cap, and speak into his ear. I point in the direction of Chattanooga. There's a row of high hills far to the east of the city, and I tell him that's my home, the place where I was raised.

And then comes the moment that I've been practicing for in my dreams. I tell Ryan about the murdered Chickasaw and the Cherokee suicide, Sautee and his lover, Nacoochee. It's a new story to him, and he smiles—then almost gives Miss Georgia a heart attack when he pretends to throw his adventure video off the cliff. I laugh, and he hands me the tape like he knows it means more to me than him, like he knows that I might actually want to sit down and watch it one day, see all those ridiculous sights that we missed seeing together.

Our guide points at a bare patch of land in the valley below us. "There was a cornfield there until a few days ago," she says. "That's where we have the Enchanted Maze."

"Please," I say to her. "Let us enjoy this."

The girl walks off in sort of a huff, and Ryan and I stay there on Lover's Leap for a long time, holding each other, savoring the view of the autumn mountains. The hardwoods are splashed orange and yellow and red, and I wonder what states we're looking at, whether you can really see far-off places like Virginia, Kentucky, the Carolinas. For some reason I doubt it, don't believe that's possible. We're sitting in Georgia, and I can recognize the hazy hilltops of Tennessee. Other than that, all I know for certain is that Ryan looks just like a young goddamn Andy, and I can see Alabama.

Alabama, 'Bama, always 'Bama.

Little Man

THE BLACK BEAR shows up in our bee yard just as I'm starting to fix breakfast for the old man. It's one of Daddy's bad mornings—one of those wipe-his-ass-for-him mornings when he doesn't know me at all—so I'm already in a sour mood when I look out the kitchen window and see the bear at the far end of the pasture, maybe two hundred yards off. She's hardly feeding, just taking apart our hives one at a time and being real destructive about it.

I brought the last of the hives back down from Georgia yesterday—pretty much everything I own in the world sits in the buzzing corner of that field. I curse and go for the .308 that I keep by the door. It pays to keep a rifle handy during deer season. You never know when a buck might show up. Coyotes too.

Now a bear, that's different. Bears are way off-limits, even in the Panhandle. But I don't know of any law against shooting *near* a bear, and besides, there's not a whole lot you can't get away with this far back in the pinewoods, living at the blind end of three miles of gravel.

I open the kitchen door and sit down on the concrete steps. The rifle is a youth-model Savage that my short ass never really grew out of. I chamber a round and find the bear in the scope, figure that I'll aim good and high, put a warning shot in the soft trunk of a pine tree growing at the edge of the field. I rest my elbows on my knees and let loose a slow, steady breath as I squeeze off.

The explosion rattles the house, and behind me I hear Daddy give a surprised yelp. I look up and see the honey-crazed bear hasn't even flinched. She's still got her face buried in a toppled hive, and between that and the sound of my daddy crying maybe I lose it just a bit. The bear stands up on her hind legs and I chamber another round, put the cross hairs right on her chest. The second shot catches her square and she stumbles back like a man, biting at the wound as if she just got stung by the mother of all bees. The bear dances round for a couple of seconds, then drops to all fours, does a couple of half jumps before collapsing for good.

So now what. I set the rifle down and go inside to my father. He's spilled corn flakes on the floor, so I clean up real quick. "Everything's fine," I tell him. "I'll be back in a few minutes." He nods without looking my way.

My brother lives alone in a trailer next to the house, and I guess he heard me shoot. I'm walking to the bee yard when Randall comes riding over on his four-wheeler. He stops next to the bear and kills the engine. "Damn," he says. "They'll put you under the jail for that, Jake." Still, I can tell that he's pleased. Where most people see trouble, Randall's likely to see an opportunity. He hops off the four-wheeler and kicks at the dead bear. "Well," he says, "let's get this girl inside before somebody wanders up on us."

"What do I want with a bear?" I ask. "Come on and help me bury her."

"Oh no, no, no," says Randall. "I can get you good money for that bear."

"What are you talking about?"

"Remember when I used to work Sparky's boat with all those Chinks?"

"Sure," I say. "So?"

"So one night me and that deck hand Quan shot a cub raiding the dumpster behind Callio's." Randall does a quick drumroll on his jeans with the flats of his hands. "Bears are like magic to those people. His grandfather gave us a thousand bucks for it."

"You never told me that."

Randall smiles wide like a prom king. "We all got secrets, little man."

I'm thinking about selling out to Glen Morgan. That's my secret. I bumped into him the other day at the bank, and one thing led to another. We talked about how lucky we were to have missed out on both Katrina and Rita, then I got to complaining about the honey business. I could see Morgan's ears perk up. He farms bees himself, is always looking to expand.

My livelihood is honey. I clear fifty, sixty grand a year, and that's not bad for around here, not bad at all. But I know that I'll never do much better, and there's always the danger that I'll do a lot worse. There's a ceiling but no real floor, so to speak. Just the other day I was reading up in a trade magazine about this new crisis spreading through Europe, this phenomenon where overnight all of the adult bees will abandon their hive and their queen for no apparent reason. I expect that'll be coming our way sooner or later. If it's not one thing it's another.

It's the rhythms of this life that, more than anything, have been wearing on me lately. The purest and best-tasting honey in the world comes from bees working the blossoms of the tupelo trees that grow in the Apalachicola River basin. But it doesn't come easy. I'm married to our bees. For the spring bloom I load my boat and station close to four hundred hives on remote docks all along the river. If I'm lucky and the weather stays right, nectar flows for about two or three bust-ass weeks and then that's it—tupelo season's over. By the end of May I move all our hives off the river and up to Georgia. Some farmers over around Lake Seminole let me run yards on their land, so through the summer our bees pollinate watermelon and cotton crops—produce a red, baker's-grade honey that keeps them healthy and helps pay the bills. After the first cold snap and the end of the cotton harvest, I'll collect the bees a second time, move them to the back pasture of our farm in Wewahitchka. I use the off-season to give them their mite treatments, and—since nothing's really blooming—I also put out corn syrup to help a bit, feed them like any other farm animal until the red maples blossom in January and the hives are ready to go back onto the river.

I reckon it was the corn syrup that brought that skinny bear. She needed to get herself fattened up for winter, and a sweet whiff of that sugar must have been more than she could resist. It's a real shame because it wasn't her fault. A bear's a slave to its nature same as us all. Still, she was messing with my rhythms, and messing with my rhythms just won't do.

At dark, Randall brings the Vietnamese man by the house to see the dead bear. Quan's about our age—thirty or so—and we've met a couple times down at the shrimp docks. I shake his thin hand, and he follows me out back to our cinder-block honey house. He's taller than me; hell, everybody's taller than me.

I've slid a steel swivel hook through a cut in the bear's hind leg, used a chain hoist to lift her off the ground. She hangs suspended from an I-beam as an empty seed sack collects the thick blood slowly dripping from her mouth. Quan sets down a small ice chest and approaches the bear, making a back-of-the-throat clucking sound as he runs his hands through her dense black fur. He turns to me and smiles. "I'll give you a thousand," he says.

I don't have a clue what a bear might be worth, but my brother—that's exactly the type of thing I'd expect him to know. I glance over at Randall standing in the shadows, see him flash three fingers. "Three thousand," I counter.

Quan frowns. "I only brought a grand."

"That's too bad," I say, knowing better than to bid against myself. "Sorry we couldn't work something out." I'm walking out the door when Quan stops me.

"Meet me at the docks tomorrow," he says. "I'll have another thousand."

Again I look to my brother, and he gives a split-the-difference shrug. Two thousand dollars ain't gonna change my life but I don't throw away money in any form. I nod and the deal is done.

Quan borrows a hacksaw, and I hold the bear steady while he cuts off all four paws. Blade meets bone with a sound like a zipper scratching. He seals the paws in plastic bags and places them in his ice chest. I spin the bear, and Quan pulls a knife from his belt, makes a small, bloodless slit along the abdomen. Rolling up his sleeve, he wiggles a hand under the rib cage and slides his arm elbow-deep into the bear. He closes his eyes as he feels around, then gives a quick twist and smiles. I hear something wet tearing inside the bear, and when Quan withdraws his bloody arm he's holding the pink gallbladder. He slices the pear-shaped gall free. "Very good," he says. "Very, very good."

I'm fetching another Ziploc when I look up and spot Daddy. Randall left the door cracked, and our father has wandered into the honey house. The fly of his pajama bottoms is unbuttoned, and I can see his shriveled penis. He's watching us work and grinning. Quan steps away from the bear, and I wince as he gives our father a deep bow.

Daddy was in Vietnam. When I was a kid, the battery in our truck exploded and he didn't speak for two days. So to see him standing there—docile as a dairy cow, smiling at the blood-stained Vietnamese stranger—that's painful, reminds me just how far gone he is from the Alzheimer's. His lips move but no real words come out. Frustrated, he stamps his bare foot down on the cold concrete.

"Randall," I say. "Go bring Daddy back to the house."

My brother looks up and notices him standing there for the first time. "Sir, yessir," he says, taking our silent father by the arm. Daddy shuffles outside, and it's not until he's left that I realize Quan's watching me with sort of a heartbroken look on his face. He pats me on the shoulder with his clean hand, and I open the plastic bag wide. He slips the gallbladder in.

After Quan leaves, Randall cuts the tenderloins out of the bear and wraps them in butcher paper for the freezer. I gather some shovels and we use the four-wheeler to take the carcass off our property, bouncing down a skidder trail until we reach an old briar-choked cutover. I've given Randall a couple of the hundreds, so he helps me scratch out a hole in the sandy soil without complaining any more than usual. For the most part we work in silence.

Randall and I have the same brown hair, flat face, and gray eyes. Other than that, we're about as different as a pair of identical twins can be. And I don't only mean on the inside. During high school, I just stopped growing for some reason. Daddy used to say it happened because I thought too much—that was his way of making me feel better when Randall called me his little brother. Whatever the cause, fact is I turned out a size smaller. Five feet to his six. I was the one stuck inside our mother when she died. I think we all wonder sometimes whether that had anything to do with it.

I reckon Randall suspects that I'm considering selling out—he jokes around the subject enough—but it's not something that we've ever really discussed. I take care of Daddy and the bees, and Randall goes on taking care of Randall. I doubt that he cares one way or the other what I do. It's all the same to him. My brother's always said he wouldn't spend his life farming bees. He's been true to his word on that one point.

I flip my shovel and toss another measure of dirt across the mutilated bear. "What do you want with that greasy meat anyway?" I ask.

"You never ate bear?"

"No, you?"

"Oh man, best thing in the world." Randall winks at me. "Tastes just like bald eagle," he says, stealing the punch line of the old poacher's joke.

From the front porch I can see the flicker of the television through our living room window. Shedding my muddy work boots, I step inside and find Daddy asleep on the couch. I cover him with a quilt and sit down by his feet, start watching this show about dating.

They've set an L.A. fellow up with four women all at the same time. They're at dinner, they're out dancing, they're drinking champagne in a steaming hot tub. He sends the girls packing one by one until finally the credits roll and it's just him and the winner. The new couple closes a door in the cameraman's face and I guess that means they fuck. What an easy world they live in. I can't imagine what my daddy would think about a show like this.

I kill the television and he sits up with a gasp, like the silence has somehow surprised him. "It's okay," I say as he pulls at his hair. "You wanna go to bed?"

Daddy shakes his head, and I watch him stare at that dead television. I swear, looking at him, you'd almost think he's trying to remember something important to tell me before he goes on back to dreaming.

I have some bear-busted hives to repair before I meet Quan, so I wake up early the next morning, leave the house carrying a hammer and a paper sack of tack nails. The frost on the field melts with the sunrise, and soon the cuffs of my jeans are soaking wet from walking through the slick green ryegrass.

One of the hives has been ripped in half. I smoke the angry bees to keep them calm, then sort through loose frames searching for the queen. I mark all my girls with a little dab of paint on the thorax and so I find her soon enough, stumbling across the cold grass like a lost drunk. I'm helping her back into the box when one of her attendants takes flight. She finds her way under my veil and stings me on the cheek. That's a tender spot so it hurts like hell. Just one more cost of doing business. I finish up with the hives and head back to the house.

Randall's in the backyard breaking up sections of dry pecan with the log splitter. He can't hear me over the motor, so I wave until he sees that I'm leaving. He's pretty good about keeping an eye on Daddy when I'm not around. I start up my truck and he shoots me the bird as a joke. That's his way of saying goodbye.

It takes me over an hour to drive down to Apalach. Easing along Water Street, I spot Quan scrubbing the deck of a fiberglass trawler. I figure that he needs some time to finish up so I make the block, stop at the Gibson Inn for a cup of coffee.

Some sport fishermen are drinking bloody marys on the

wraparound porch of the Gibson. They say hello as I pass and I smile at their outfits: the identical pairs of polarized sunglasses, flats gear from Orvis and Columbia worth more than all the clothes in my closet.

It's turned into a nice crisp day, so I take my coffee back outside and sit down on the wooden steps. The four fishermen are lined up in rocking chairs behind me, and I listen as they argue over the perfect tarpon fly, the best way to spot a tailing redfish.

"Here he comes," says one of the fishermen. I look up and see Archie rounding the corner. The old black man showed up in town a few days after the storm flooded New Orleans; people say he has a sister here, living somewhere near the tracks. He stops at the pay phone across the street and checks the coin return for change. This is something Archie does maybe two or three times an hour as he makes his wandering rounds through town. The fishermen have picked up on the rhythm of his routine and are laughing at him. "Watch this," the heaviest one says after Archie ambles off.

The fat man jogs across the street, and the sun flaps that are on the back of his long-billed cap bounce like a beagle's ears. He stops at the pay phone and makes a big show of opening his wallet. I see him tuck a few bills into the change slot before he turns back around. The other fishermen are roaring with laughter as their buddy waddles up the porch steps.

"Gonna make that old boy's day," he says, a little out of breath from the effort.

Twenty minutes later, I'm finishing up my coffee when Archie comes around again. The fishermen giggle as he shuffles down the sidewalk. He's drinking a brown-bagged beer and already there's a wobble to his walk. Archie approaches the pay phone, and someone behind me says that this oughtta be good.

The old man does a funny thing when he finds the money. I guess his first thought is that someone has gone and stuffed trash into the pay phone because he throws the bills down on the concrete. He's starting to walk away when something clicks and he stops. He kneels down for a better look, and the fat fisherman says, "Well, looky here," in a fake deep voice.

Standing, Archie sees us white men sitting on the porch and freezes. "This y'all's money?" he hollers. I look away as Archie takes a long pull from his beer.

"What money?" two of the fishermen say at once.

Archie wipes his mouth on the sleeve of his flannel shirt and studies us for a bit. We stay quiet as he shrugs and pockets the cash. The fishermen keep their poker faces until he disappears around the corner, then the fat one says, "This y'all's money?" and they all start cackling as if pissing away money is the funniest thing that a man could ever do.

I leave the truck parked at the Gibson while I walk over to the shrimp docks to see Quan. He's finished washing the trawler, and I find him sitting alone on the trunk of a Nissan, smoking a cigarette. He looks so happy and relaxed that I almost hate to bother him.

He smiles when he spots me crossing the street. "Hey, Jake," he says, hopping to his feet like a gymnast. We shake hands and he removes a folded bank envelope from the front pocket of his shirt. "More hundreds," he says. "Figured that'd be easier for you to count."

"Yeah, sure." I check the envelope before cramming it into my torn canvas wallet. "Guess I'll see you around."

"Wait." Quan pulls a tiny vial from his sock and places it in my palm. "Here," he says.

I study the dark green fluid trapped in the glass cylinder. "This what I think it is?"

"Pure bear bile," he whispers. "Grandfather extracted a tiny bit last night after I told him about Mr. George."

"Jesus." I shoot a nervous glance down Water Street. "All I need is to get caught with this shit."

"It's a gift," says Quan. "He said you should try giving some to your father."

"The hell I will."

"It might help him," he says, stepping away. "Please take it."

Quan drives off before I can change my mind, so I put the vial in my pocket and stroll on back to the Gibson. I'm crossing the street when I see that the fishermen have placed an open bottle of wine on top of Archie's pay phone. The more I think about it, the more it pisses me off.

I back my truck across the road and onto the sidewalk. It's a struggle, but I'm able to stretch my short arm out of the open window just far enough to grab the bottle off the pay phone. Angry fishermen howl from the porch, and I switch into first, roll past them trailing red wine like blood from an open wound. The bottle empties and I toss it into the bed of my truck.

All of this makes me feel a little better, but I'm pretty sure I know what old Archie would say if he'd seen the show. He'd say, Don't do me any more favors, son—I've never even had a sip of decent wine.

I pass Glen Morgan's place on my way back to Wewa and pull off the highway. The brand-new Dodge dually parked in his yard is painted Cat yellow and sports happy-honeybee decals on both doors. I can't help but laugh. Morgan's not a bad guy at all, but I swear he farms bees like he's some kind of oil man.

Tupelo Gold, Incorporated, accounts for about half of the five hundred barrels of commercial tupelo honey harvested every spring. That makes Morgan's operation around ten times bigger than mine. He's forever wanting more, and I imagine that's what all his phone calls have been about. I figure it's high time that I talked to the man—no harm in hearing him out.

My old man and Morgan used to be pretty good friends, but Daddy would still badmouth him behind his back just a bit, say that he didn't have enough pride in his product. And it's true, Morgan does take a few shortcuts here and there. I go through the trouble to haul our hives into the swamp for a reason. Out on the river, the waterlocked bees don't have anything to drink but blooming tupelo. But Morgan won't fool with boats. His yards are on the high-ground edges of the swamp, and sure, his bees find plenty of tupelo—but they're also sucking on the gall-berries blooming over in the hardwoods about that same time of year. His honey suffers for that.

Morgan comes out onto the porch just as I'm parking next to his ridiculous truck. He's holding a picture book and has a granddaughter cradled in his big arms. When he sees that it's me, he smiles and sets the girl down carefully like he's releasing a bass. She runs back into the house with her book, and he comes down the steps to meet me.

"Hello there, Jake," he says. "Tried calling you the other day."

"I thought it might be better if I just came by." We shake hands, and I see my fingers are stained red from the spilled wine. "Hope I didn't catch you in the middle of anything."

"No, course not," he says. "How's Georgie getting along?"

"About the same, I guess."

"Well, y'all are in our prayers."

"Yessir. Thank you."

Morgan nods and scratches his neck. "Let's take a walk," he says. "I'll show you my latest hobby."

I follow him around the house to an old goat pen that runs

alongside his barn. There's a little tin shelter in the corner. Morgan claps his hands, and I hear a sharp bark as two hound-size deer come bouncing on out. They crowd up against the hog-wire fence, and I see the male has tiny forked antlers, the tusks of a wild hog.

"What the hell are those?" I ask.

"Muntjacs," says Morgan. "From India or Asia or something. I went to buy peacocks off a fellow in Alabama and ended up with these guys. I just love 'em."

"What do you do with them?"

"I'm hoping to breed this pair." Morgan tears a handful of clover from the ground and sprinkles it over the fence for the muntjacs. "They'll eat meat too, you know."

"Come on."

"No kidding. Wait here."

Morgan disappears into the barn, then returns wearing mule-skin work gloves and carrying a trap-killed rat. "Watch this," he says, tossing the dead rat into the pen.

The buck muntjac is the first to reach the rat. He snatches it into his mouth and does a victory lap around the pen with the doe trailing behind him. "Holy shit," I say.

Morgan chuckles as he shakes off his rat gloves. I watch the muntjacs fight over the rat for a long while before I realize that he is staring at me. "Here's the deal," he says. "Go ahead and make an inventory of all your equipment, all your bee leases, whatever else you can think of. I'll make a real good offer if you'll sign a no-compete."

"What, you gonna start working the river?"

He shakes his head. "Oh no, not me," he says, spitting over the fence. "Look, Jake, there's only a handful of people left in the world that know how to make tupelo honey, right?"

"I guess."

"My father taught me—and your father, God bless him, he

taught you." Morgan waves a hand across the sky. "Ain't nobody gonna just move down here and start doing this for a living."

I nod so he'll know that I'm listening, but I'm also still watching the muntjacs. They're tugging at the dead rat, and its hide has begun to tear. The doe jerks her head, and the rat's ropy gray intestines spill out onto the dust of the goat pen.

Morgan keeps on. "I'll be dead straight with you," he says. "There's nothing you have that I really need. But I buy you out, that's one less competitor for TGI." He kicks at the fence and seems embarrassed. "Just think about it, okay?"

"Yessir," I say. "I'll think about it."

"That's all I ask." Morgan points at the muntjacs. "Watch that guy." The buck has won the battle over the rat. A naked tail is still sticking out from between his tusks when he runs over and starts trying to mount the tiny doe. Morgan laughs. "They really are something."

Randall is stacking firewood when I make it back to the house. Daddy has joined him outside and sits on a stump watching. I walk up behind my father and put a hand on his shoulder. He doesn't even flinch, just rolls his head back and smiles as if he's been expecting me all along. The old man truly does live a life without surprises. Most days we have that in common.

"How goes it?" says Randall.

I decide to come clean and tell him about Morgan. He piles pecan until I finish talking, then wipes the sweat from his face with the front of his shirt. "So what do you plan on doing for a living, Jake?"

I shrug. "I don't know," I say. "This and that, I guess. Like you."

Randall picks up a loose piece of wood. "It's not as easy as it looks," he says. "This and that."

"Maybe."

Randall laughs. "How about that, Daddy?" he says. "Jake's thinking about helping Glen Morgan corner the market."

I tell Randall to shut his damn mouth. Deer dogs strike up in the distant timber, and I rub our father's big shoulders until he goes on back to grinning.

In the evening, I sit down in the kitchen with Daddy and watch him eat some of the stew that I've heated up. He's getting it down pretty good on his own, but every now and then I have to lean over and wipe off his chin for him.

One of Randall's pretty girlfriends stopped by right before dark, and I can hear music and laughter coming from his trailer. I think maybe Daddy hears the music too because he's tapping his feet on the linoleum and, far as I can tell, keeping good time.

My aunt always told me that he was a dancer—that there was a time when my parents would drive over to a club in Tallahassee every couple weeks. Still, I never saw any dancing out of him before now. It could just be the Alzheimer's.

The bear bile's still in my pocket and I get to daydreaming, imagining that it actually works—that I slip it into his milk before bed and wake up the next morning to the smell of bacon cooking. Daddy's in the kitchen waving a spatula and giving Randall shit. But he smiles when he sees me. He says, Good morning, son, and asks how many eggs I want for breakfast. Later, we leave my brother to clean the dishes and head out to the bee yard. Daddy inspects the hives real carefully, then slaps me on the back, says I did a real good job taking care of everything while he was away. We put in a long, hard day together—me and Daddy getting the bees ready for winter—but the work isn't quite as hard nor near as lonely as it has been without him.

It's a silly thing to hope for—a child's dream, really. In the end, all I do is hide that little glass vial in my sock drawer, knowing that it will stay there forever, that the bear bile will still be sitting next to my stacks of *Playboy* when spring comes, the tupelos bloom, and I am alone in the river swamp, working my father's bees.

Winter

Winter

Borderlands

HIS SETTER FOUND her in a cold canebrake, half-buried in the loam, her mouth sealed with duct tape. Wes saw that it was her, Sara Champagne. Three fingers had been cut from her right hand, two from her left. She was naked to the waist, and a thin red tear ran from the base of her throat and then down across her belly.

Wes whistled soft for Sally. She bumped the steaming corpse with her nose, then gave a sad whine before coming to heel. The breeze died and a hawk screamed; something moved in the thicket. Through a break in the switch cane Wes saw a lank man in beaded buckskins rise and begin to move away. At fifteen yards the pale stranger turned and flashed a guilty smile. Wes fired both barrels of his 20-gauge, then ran for the levee with Sally clipping at his heels.

"Look," said Comeaux. "Duck cop."

Wes sat in his uncle's city-police cruiser, and together they watched a line of parish deputies come fishtailing down the gravel road that ran alongside the levee. Trailing behind them all was a game warden in a green Dodge Ram.

Comeaux tapped at the steering wheel while the deputies parked and piled out. "So," he said to Wes, "just one more time. That man came at you, right?"

"Yessir."

"Don't say nothing else. Understand?"

Wes nodded.

"Hell of a Sunday morning." Comeaux sighed and then opened his door. "Let's go."

His uncle knew most of the parish deputies and had a good ten years on even the oldest of them. They gathered around as the game warden produced a map of the batture, that stretch of land that ran between the levee and the Atchafalaya. Wes showed the spot as best he could, and then a deputy handed him a cheerleader-on-one-knee photograph, a pretty girl smiling. Wes flinched. "I already told y'all that it was Sara Champagne," he said. "I knew her."

Before long the sheriff himself arrived in a red Z71. The tall man was still in his church clothes, and they waited as he swapped his loafers for a pair of rubber knee-boots that he kept in his diamond-plated truck box. He nodded at Comeaux. "Hey, Pistol Pete."

"Hey," said Comeaux.

The sheriff shook Comeaux's hand and was introduced to Wes. The deputies all stepped aside as the sheriff looked him over. "How old are you, son?"

"Seventeen."

"You in school?"

"Yessir. I'm a senior at Livonia."

"You're a big kid. You play football?"

"No, sir."

The sheriff pointed at Comeaux. "Did you know he was my center back in high school?"

"No."

"Tell him, Petey."

"It's true," said Comeaux.

The sheriff studied Wes. "You should have played ball."

"All right." Wes saw Comeaux narrow his eyes, his way of telling him not to be a smart-ass. "Yessir," Wes added. "A lot of people say that."

"I bet." The sheriff tucked the cuffs of his gray dress pants down into his LaCrosses, then rose up again. "So you were bird hunting?"

"Yessir. Woodcock."

"Using what? Eights? Nines?"

"Seven and a halfs."

"For woodcock?"

"Sometimes we jump rabbits down there."

The game warden laughed. "You're gonna ruin that bird dog," he said. "Make a beagle out of him."

"He's a meat dog," said Wes. "He gets it."

The sheriff sliced his hand through the air, and they quieted. "How far away was he?"

Wes pointed over at Sally, asleep in the sun. "Maybe me to her."

"And what are your chokes in that side-by-side?"

"Improved, then modified."

"Where'd you aim?"

"I don't really remember," said Wes. "I might not of aimed."

The sheriff let his head roll back as he thought all that over. "Okay," he said finally. "Stay put for now."

A call was sent out, and soon backup came steadily pouring in along the gravel road that led from the highway. More parish deputies and more game wardens, city cops like Comeaux from Livonia and Fordoche, Morganza and Krotz Springs. State troopers, even. Wes watched them load riot shotguns and AR-15s, then space themselves out along the levee for as far as he could see. One man every fifty yards or so. The sheriff stood atop his truck box and shouted orders. He hollered down to Comeaux, said that boats were already patrolling the river in case their killer went a-swimming.

They waited more than an hour for the dog team from the state penitentiary to arrive, then turned the Angola bloodhounds loose next to a van one of the game wardens found parked near the railroad tracks. Men fanned out into the batture, and later Wes listened as the sheriff shared a cigarette with Comeaux and talked. "We came across him laid out in the cane," said the sheriff. "Face so full of birdshot it looks like God cursed him."

"Dead?"

"Oh yeah," said the sheriff. "A couple of pellets clipped his jugular. You should see the fucking blood, Petey."

Wes saw a young deputy standing alone atop the levee. He had puked down the front of his uniform and was cleaning himself off with a towel. Wes stared at him until it clicked. He remembered that same man circling their house holding divorce papers last summer, his father screaming that he'd never open the door.

Comeaux took a long drag, then whispered to the sheriff through his fingers. "Find a gun?" he asked.

The sheriff shook his head. "Just the biggest knife you ever saw. Chef knife. Sharp as a gar's tooth." He smiled. "Don't worry. The boy did right."

The sheriff ambled off, and Comeaux looked over at Wes. "You okay with all this?" he asked.

"I guess so," said Wes. "I'm not in any trouble?"

"Hell, no. You're a hero."

Wes waited for his uncle to laugh, but he didn't. "Do me a favor, nonc?"

"What's that?"

"Don't tell my mother about none of this, okay? I'll tell her myself. I'll tell her when I'm ready."

She rang him at dusk. She'd do that when she knew his father wasn't home to answer. Wes was short with her and didn't mention finding Sara, killing a man. She paused, regrouped, asked if he'd been studying for his exams. He told her that school had let out for Christmas, that she'd know that if she hadn't left.

His mother went quiet, and Wes slipped the heavy phone into its cradle. He stayed in the kitchen waiting for her to call back, but she didn't and so after a while he stepped outside to watch the day fade.

Sally bounced around her kennel like a dancing bear, whining for another hunt. Wes ignored her and wandered to the back of the lot. He looked out over the neighbor's pasture. A herd of Brahma-crossed swamp cows lazed in the darkening ryegrass, and in a far corner an oil well older than Wes kept at its seesaw rhythm, sucking on that muddy field like a great steel mosquito.

What media came looking were blocked by Comeaux. He told them that the boy was gone, had up and moved away. In the end they kept his name out of the papers on account of his age, but no secrets last in Livonia. Wes lay low for a few days, then, Wednesday morning, ducked into Penny's for coffee and toast. He saw that the poster of Sara had been taken off the back of the cash register. The missing girl had been found.

A stir in the diner: nods, sad smiles, and winks. Wes turned to leave and there was Celia Trahan, strawberry lips asking if he planned on making the wake. Wes glanced down at his worn jeans, his flannel shirt. "We'll see," he said.

Celia caught his meaning. "You have some nice clothes, don't you?"

"I guess."

"Great." She bit down on her bottom lip. "Maybe you could ride with me, okay?"

Wes hesitated, then brushed his shaggy hair out of his eyes. "Sure," he said.

"You live right there off the highway, don't you?"

"Yeah."

"By the tire yard?"

"By the tire yard."

"Good. I'll pick you up at five o'clock."

Celia kissed his cheek, and he felt his ears go red. She backed away, then a pool of girls absorbed her like a bead of mercury. As they went bubbling out the door, some asshole in a booth clapped. He was an out-of-town trucker, didn't know the score. An old waitress hushed him and said, You be quiet, them poor kids just lost one of they friends.

LAKE CITY: THE GATEWAY TO FLORIDA. A dog-eared post-card addressed to him by way of Comeaux. No return address, but Wes already had that memorized, saw it on the papers that the deputy had finally managed to serve on his father. Wes flipped the postcard over. *Thinking of you. Things are crazy now, but you'll understand one day. Have a wonderful and blessed Christmas. Love, Mom.*

Sally went to barking as Wes pulled on his father's only suit. He heard a knock, then the front door opening. Wes cursed. "I'll be right there," he said. "Just give me one second." He ran a wet comb through his hair, stepped out of the bathroom with a tie slung across his shoulder.

Celia was waiting for him in the living room. Her black dress was printed with white orchids. "You living here by yourself?" she asked.

"Half the time. Daddy works fourteens offshore."

"I'm sorry about your mama."

"Thanks." A stray drop of water escaped from Wes's damp hair and ran down across his face. He wiped it away with his hand.

Celia grinned at him. "Think I could have a beer?"

"Yeah, sure. There's some in the icebox."

"I figured."

"Right. Sorry." Wes led her into the kitchen and winced at the dishes piled high in the sink. He opened two High Lifes with the front of his clean shirt and handed her one.

"What was it like?" asked Celia.

"What?"

"Finding Sara, shooting that fucker?"

Wes shrugged and tried to wiggle his toes inside his father's black shoes, a size too small. "I can't really say."

Celia frowned but told him that she understood. She tilted her beer toward him. "To Sara," she said.

"Sara." Their bottles clicked, and they both took a long pull.

Celia set her beer on the kitchen table and lifted the tie from his shoulder. She placed it around her own neck. "Come closer," she ordered. He shuffled to her and she grabbed hold of his lapels, began to struggle with the top button of his dress shirt. "Damn, big guy, when was the last time you wore this?"

"I ain't never wore it."

"Well, you're too big for it," she said. "You'll just have to wear it open, without a tie."

"That all right?"

"Absolutely," she told him. "That's what all the celebrities are doing now anyways."

The smell, that biology-lab smell, it stunned Wes like a slap. He stepped back, and Celia caught him by the elbow. She led him to the coffin as teenagers whispered. A boy named Chris he'd hated his whole life stepped forward to touch Wes on the arm, tell him good job.

Sara's dress was crushed velvet, ink black with lace frills. A broad white ribbon had been tied across her waist, and makeup cracked at the corners of her mouth. Wes studied her: the lipstick different, the bangs wrong. Her hands disappeared into a spray of roses resting on her lap. He remembered missing fingers and shivered like a rabbit when Celia squeezed his own sweaty hand.

Wes sat outside Gene's Hardware watching feral cats battle over trash. They screamed like devils, and so he bounced an old battery off the dumpster to quiet them. He'd taken off the black shoes and his thin socks, was massaging his swollen feet when Comeaux's cruiser finally pulled up. His uncle leaned out the open window. "Well," he said. "You coming?"

Wes stuffed his socks into one of the shoes and picked his way barefoot to the cruiser. "Sorry, nonc. I didn't have anyone else to call."

"No problem," said Comeaux. "Hop in."

Wes folded himself into the passenger seat of the Crown Vic. "Thanks," he said.

"Sure." Comeaux made a wide turn in the parking lot, and they headed back toward Livonia with the sunset off their left shoulders. "It's nothing to be ashamed of," he said.

"I ain't ashamed."

"Looks to me like you've been beating yourself up a little. Maybe I'm wrong."

"I'm just mad I ever agreed to go in the first place."

"Celia Trahan is a pretty girl."

"Yes, she is." Wes leaned his head against the cool window. "They both were."

"True enough." Comeaux punched the cigarette lighter. "And so where's she now?"

"Still inside, I guess."

Comeaux grunted and followed the highway along the bayou. A woodcock flew low over the road, leaving the shore thicket to night-hunt earthworms in open fields. Wes lost it in the horizon, then turned and caught Comeaux watching him.

"Your mama called me today," said Comeaux. "She wants to talk to you."

"Got a funny way of showing it."

"She had to leave. You know that."

"No, I don't."

His uncle told him to settle down and listen. "My own mama married two very different men," he said. "The first one —my daddy—he was nice, maybe even a little weak." Comeaux glanced over at Wes. "He died when I was about your age."

"And then came Paw-paw."

"That's right," said Comeaux. "The second one—Sidney, your grandfather—he was a mean motherfucker."

"Yeah," said Wes. "I remember that about him."

"Well, your daddy takes after Sidney in a whole lot of ways that I'm not so sure he can help." Comeaux shook his head. "I didn't do a very good job looking after Bones when he was a kid."

Wes shrugged and kept quiet until they pulled into his gravel driveway. "Thanks for the ride," he said.

"He still on the rig?"

"Till Sunday. Christmas."

Comeaux spit into an empty Coke can. "Just think about calling her. All I ask."

"Yessir." Wes grabbed the black shoes and turned to his uncle. "You mind feeding Sally for a couple days?"

"Where you going?"

"The houseboat, maybe."

"Go get your mind right. I'll take care of her."

Wes opened the door of the cruiser and hesitated. "You killed, right? Back when you were in the army?"

The police scanner squawked, and the cherry of Comeaux's Winston went bright in the final moments of dusk. "Yeah," he said, "a few." He stared at Wes for a long while before exhaling. "None of them deserved dying as much as that son of a bitch you shot did. Remember that, okay?"

Wes stood in the front yard by the satellite dish. He watched Comeaux back out onto the highway, then head for town. Twilight gave way to a cold, dark night as he lingered. Sally howled from her kennel at a far-off siren, and from up high came the faint racket of snow geese, invisible flocks beating their way south just ahead of a front.

He awoke on the couch with her standing over him. The white orchids on her dress were floating like tiny ghosts in the dim room. Wes reached for her, pulled her onto his nest of quilts until she was lying alongside him. A soft thump, then another, shoes dropping to the floor. She was on top of him now, her dress gathered thigh high as she moved over his body. Wes slid his hand along the inside of her leg, and she gave a surprised giggle. She kissed him lightly, smoothed his hair before rolling away.

"Slow down, there, tiger."

"Sorry." His voice caught in his throat, and she smiled. She began stroking his stomach beneath the quilt.

"I looked all over for you," she said.

"I called my uncle for a ride. I should have told you that I was leaving."

She leaned back against him, her head resting on his shoulder. "So what happened?"

"It just got to me, being that close to her again. I felt like I couldn't breathe." From outside, he heard the double clutch of a rig leaving town. "I'm sorry."

"Don't be sorry."

He covered her with the quilt and she nestled closer, one leg draped over his own. In a moment they were both asleep, and at dawn she was gone, leaving only a napkin note she'd clipped with a bobby pin to the waistband of his boxers. *Midnight curfew, had to run. Call me. Love, C.*

Wes had been just one night alone at the houseboat on False River before he phoned her. He asked that she miss the funeral and come see him instead. Celia hesitated but then agreed, and after an hour he went outside to wait for her.

His houseboat was the sixth in a line of ten counting from the southwest end of the oxbow lake. Wes sat on the dock and stared out across the water at the opposite shore. Three hundred years ago the Mississippi had changed course for good, leaving this twenty-two-mile meander cut off and landlocked. A false river. They called the big fist of land between the lake and the river the Island, but it wasn't really, not anymore. There was a honk, and Wes looked away. Celia's yellow Mustang was turning off the highway.

She was wearing old blue jeans and an LSU sweatshirt. He

gave her a spare jacket that had belonged to his mother, and they took his johnboat to the South Flats. At the edge of Bayou Jarreau he showed her how to throw the cast net for shiners, and together they baited a little twenty-hook trotline that he ran between two prop-scarred cypress knees. Later Celia told him to relax while she fixed lunch, and he said, Thanks, I need to run and get gas for the outboard anyway.

The gas station was on the Island. Wes drove east to circle around to the back side of the crescent lake, and on the way he passed a ripe patch of sugar cane, just burned and ready to cut. A battered harvester mowed the standing cane down by the row, and a tractor drawing a high-sided trailer kept time, collecting the blur of billet that dropped from the elevator.

Wes pulled his pickup onto the side of the road not far from where half a dozen black kids had gathered, sucking sugar stalks and waiting. The boys ignored him, and the harvester doubled back, began to mow the last of the rows. They fanned out along the highway armed with clubs and pellet guns and broken asphalt. Behind the harvester a hundred egrets worked the cut field, chicken-scratching the stubble for field mice and lizards.

As the fifth row fell, they came. Rabbits—cottontails and swampers both—exploded from the blackened cane, darting across the highway for the shelter of a new green field. The boys went serious and clubbed what they could as the smallest child moved among them, dispatching the wounded rabbits with six pumps on his rusty Benjamin and a point-blank headshot.

They worked under the orders of an older boy. Shirtless in the chill air, he swung a three-foot length of rebar like a bush hook, sending rabbits tumbling with pendulum-smooth strokes. Great clouds of ash, cold and gray, swirled like dust devils across the highway. In the distance Wes could see coal smoke from Big Cajun II collecting in the oily winter sky. He cranked up the Ford and went on his way, following Island Road.

When he returned to the houseboat, Celia told him that she had changed her mind, that she wanted to go to the funeral after all. "And I want you to come with me," she said. "I want us to go together."

They were sitting across from each other at the kitchen table. She'd made a plate of ham sandwiches on white bread, but neither of them was feeling hungry. "I don't think so," said Wes.

"Because of what happened at the wake?"

"Sure."

"If things get weird again, just tell me. I'll help see you through it."

"Things will get weird."

"Then talk to me about it. I can't help unless you open up some." Celia stood and circled around the table until she was standing behind him. Her belt buckle pressed against his skull, and he pushed back against it. She put her hands on his shoulders and rubbed them. "Please come with me," she said. "I have to go."

"Why can't you just stay here with me?"

"She was my friend, Wes. She was your friend too."

"She barely knew me." He leaned forward, and Celia's hands fell from his shoulders. "You barely knew me."

"That's not true."

"Fine. We were best friends, you and me and Sara."

Wes heard Celia step away from him. He turned and saw that she was just standing there watching him with glassy eyes. Wes said nothing, and it was not until she drove off crying that he finally became hungry. He ate all of her sandwiches, then spent the rest of the night drinking Old Crow neat, broke down crying himself after he found an old pack of his mother's menthols, lost between sofa cushions.

On Christmas Eve, Comeaux came. The screen door of the houseboat slammed, and Wes jerked awake. "Christ, nonc. You scared the shit out of me."

"Santa's here," said Comeaux.

"Great."

"You look like hell. Solve your problems?"

Wes shook his stunned head. "No."

"Never does."

Comeaux went into the kitchen and Wes lay on the couch, listening as his uncle banged around. He rubbed at his eyes, then called out. "So what are you doing here?"

"Your little girl flagged me down this morning. She's worried about you, said you were acting funny yesterday."

Wes sat up. "Oh."

"She's sweet," said Comeaux. "You be nice to her."

"Yessir."

"Coffee?"

"Black."

"Tough guy."

Wes rocked forward onto his feet. "What time is it, anyway?"

"Almost noon."

"Damn."

Comeaux poured coffee into big styrofoam cups, and they took the johnboat on a slow idle across the lake, back into the stand of flooded timber where the trotline was set. The caught catfish were rolling in the daylight, and the line trembled like a guitar string. "Well, all right," said Comeaux.

His uncle kept the hooks clear of the boat while Wes col-

lected three nice channel cats. He slipped them one at a time
into a five-gallon bucket, and Comeaux pointed at all the clean
hooks. "If you'd have made it out here at dawn you'd have three
times that."

"I know," said Wes. He yanked on the pull cord, and on the
fourth try the outboard sputtered and then started.

They tied the johnboat off at the dock, and Wes climbed
out. He went into the houseboat to grab a fillet knife, and when
he returned Comeaux was standing over the white bucket of
catfish. His uncle took the knife from him. "I'll do it," he said.
"Nurse your hangover."

"You sure?"

"I'm sure."

Wes said thanks and sat down on his heels. "I need to tell
you something."

"What's that?" Comeaux tapped a Winston loose from a
crumpled soft pack and lit it off a paper book of matches. He
looked over at Wes. "Go on," he said.

"That man never came at me or nothing. He just smiled,
and I was so scared I shot him."

Comeaux lifted an eel-slick catfish by the mouth, then
pushed its bottom lip through the timber tie that Wes's father
had nailed into a piling long ago. "I understand," said Comeaux.
"In the war I saw things, did things, that I never thought I'd
shake."

"That's kinda how I feel about this," said Wes. "Like I ain't
never been so scared."

Comeaux's head bounced, and with the knife he made two
shallow cuts, one on either side of the catfish's dorsal fin. "You
know, I spent a few months in Korea between tours."

"Yeah?"

"Right on their DMZ. Most beautiful place you ever saw. An

Eden, really. We'd go on these bullshit keep-sharp patrols and see all kinds of deer, moon bears. We'd even cut tiger tracks."

"Tigers?"

"No shit. Ain't but about two miles wide, but it was like you were on another planet. They say it's still that way." Comeaux plier-peeled great strips of gray skin from the impaled catfish. "There's peace to be found in this world, Wes. You just have to look."

The channel cat hung naked on the nail, gills still working steadily as Comeaux began to cut out the fillets. Wes watched it suffer and bleed. "I guess," he said.

Wes parked at the levee and walked down into the frosted batture. A mourners' path had formed over the past week, snaking its way around the blowdowns and snags left by Katrina and then Rita. Wes followed fresh tracks through the thicket to the spot where he had found her. The switch cane was trampled flat and littered with cigarette butts. Someone had nailed a tragedy wreath to the side of a sycamore, and flowers were piled high around the base of the tree. Up above, evergreen clouds of mistletoe floated in bare branches.

He knelt opposite the memorial and tried to forget the shattered girl, remember Sara as he had known her. Trade tape-bound lips for beautiful smiles, heal her torn skin. He stayed as long as that took, and when he quit the moonlit clearing he could almost hear her laughing on a Friday-night tailgate, a wine cooler pinned between her golden knees. She's teasing Wes, calling him Elvis for his sideburns, swinging her feet as she sips on her bottle and a warm southern breeze pulls at her hair.

Wes was late for Mass and so he stood behind the last pew, searching for Celia. The congregation passed candles as they began to sing "Silent Night," and finally he spotted her near the front with her family. She turned to kindle her mother's candle and frowned when she saw him, showed him her back as the lights went dim in the Immaculate Heart of Mary. On a table near the altar sat a picture of Sara. Someone handed Wes a candle of his own, and he sang as best he could. The priest locked eyes with him, and Wes looked away.

He caught up with her in the midnight parking lot, peeling her away from her family before they all piled into a shiny sedan. She was wearing a red plaid skirt and a white sweater. Her lipstick was darker than usual, the color of oxblood leather. "Can we talk?" he asked.

Celia cocked her head, half closed her green eyes. "What do you want?"

"To apologize."

"Okay."

"I'm sorry about yesterday," he said.

"That it?"

"Well, yeah, I guess."

Celia slapped him on his arm. "Have a great Christmas." She turned and began walking to her car, her family.

"Wait." Wes grabbed her hand, and she let herself be spun around. "There's something else," he told her. "I'm leaving for a while, probably won't be back until school starts."

Celia softened. "Are you crying?"

"Forget it."

"You are." She put her hand against his jaw. "Where are you going?" she asked. "Tell me."

"Florida. To see my mom."

"Really?"

"Yeah." Wes kicked at a pebble, and it went skittering across the parking lot. "And you could come with me, you know."

Celia laughed. "You see the big man sitting in that car?" Wes looked over and saw that Mr. Trahan had his neck craned around and was watching them. Her father tapped twice on the horn as if he'd been listening in. Celia laughed again. "Daddy's kinda expecting me for Christmas," she said.

"Right."

"He'd catch us before we hit Biloxi."

"I know you can't. I just wanted to say it."

"And I'm glad that you did." Celia leaned in and hugged him. A horn blared; she drew back. "I'm sorry too," she said.

"About what?"

"I've been thinking. Praying."

"Praying?"

Celia nodded. "You weren't all wrong. I wasn't doing the things I was doing for the right reasons."

Wes tried then to kiss her on her painted lips, but she put a hand flat against his chest and stopped him. "So what does that mean?" he asked.

"It means that I want to be your friend," said Celia. "But for real this time." She held out her hand and crinkled her nose. "Friends?"

Wes left at daybreak with Sally spread out next to him on the bench seat. The traffic eased as Christmas settled in, and he made good time. This was his first trip outside of Louisiana since before the storms. He shook his head at the destruction in Mississippi, casino billboard after casino billboard corkscrewed and twisted.

Somewhere in the pine-tree wilderness between Pensacola and Tallahassee, Wes crossed the broad Apalachicola and entered a new time zone. He pulled onto the shoulder of the interstate for a piss, was unzipping his jeans when Sally bolted out the open door before he could collar her. A minivan blew by, missing the setter by a yard as she disappeared into the thin stretch of pinewoods separating the east and west lanes of I-10. Wes hollered, but Sally wasn't listening. He sprinted after her.

This was new country for them both—pine forest, cool and quiet. Sally was quartering for scent when Wes caught up to her, damn near tackled her. They fell in a heap at the base of a gnarled Torreya, that biblical gopher wood.

Wes lay back on the carpet of pine needles, holding Sally close as she licked at his face. From both sides of the forest came the occasional whine of cars cruising the interstate, tires humming on asphalt. He relaxed and listened, not to the cars, but to the stillness between the cars. He could smell the river, thick and clean, and in the treetops a nuthatch flittered back and forth, afraid to cross that open road, afraid to leave the harmony of the softwoods.

East Texas

COLSON SIPPED black coffee at a corner booth and waited for his brother's wife. Outside, a cold shower fell, flooding the cracked-asphalt canyons that spider-webbed the parking lot of the crowded diner. Broken cigarettes sailed on pothole lakes, dividing diesel rainbows. Colson flinched as a pregnant waitress shouted an order at the line cook. His jeans were wet and he shivered.

A red hatchback pulled off the highway, and Shannon poured out of the old Geo before Deb could finish parking. Colson smiled watching his niece. She was coltish still—all knees and elbows—but already pretty like her mother. She was wearing the pink jacket he had bought her for Christmas. It was brighter than he remembered, even in the rain.

Deb was in her supermarket uniform. She shielded her short black hair with a newspaper and hawk-snatched Shannon's hand. Laughing, they splashed across the parking lot and made their way inside. A trucker said, Hey, mama, and Colson stood to greet them. He hugged Shannon hard, then kissed Deb on the cheek. Her skin was damp and cool. The rain had complicated her cheap perfume, and she smelled like gardenias torn by a storm.

"Thanks for coming." Colson slid into the booth opposite Deb, and Shannon pushed in next to him, throwing her arm around his neck like a monkey.

"Of course." Deb brushed the hair from her face, exposing a smudge of printer's ink just above her left eyebrow. "So how you liking driving a tow truck?"

"I like it fine," said Colson. "I'm on my own for the most part."

Deb smiled. "And I imagine that suits you."

Colson shrugged as he handed Shannon a dollar. "Go and check out that jukebox," he told her. "Play us some songs."

Shannon scrambled out of the booth and Deb smirked. "I wish your brother was as generous with his money."

"I saw him yesterday," said Colson. "He wanted me to ask that you stop by sometime."

"You tell him I'll never bring my child into that place."

"I think he'll get that. But he'd still like to see you."

"I don't have a say?"

"I ain't pretending it's any of my business." Colson put his elbows on the table and made twin tornados with his hands. "I just promised him I'd ask so here I am."

"Twenty years, Colson. That's older than you are now." The rain stopped, and, softer, Deb added, "My job in life is to raise that little girl, not make his time easier."

Colson nodded and then fished out the five twenties that were folded in the front pocket of his work shirt. His sister-in-law watched him slide the cash across the smooth table and sighed. "I can't keep on taking your money," she said.

"I want you to have it." Colson tapped the bills closer and closer until she had no choice but to grab them before they slipped off the edge of the table.

"Thanks." Deb squeezed his wrist, letting her fingers linger before she tucked the money into her purse. "It helps," she said. "It really does."

"Course it does."

"Cut him loose," said Deb. "He poisons everything he touches."

Colson started to speak but just then Shannon came racing over from the jukebox. Her hands were balled into tiny fists and he could tell that she was angry. "Yeah?" he asked.

Shannon stomped her foot. "That damn jukebox stole my dollar."

"Watch your mouth," said Deb.

Lately small things like this could sometimes make his niece go psychotic. Their Christmas had been a disaster. Deb hooked a finger in Shannon's belt loop and tried to calm her. "You can listen to all the music you want in the car, sweetie."

"No," said Shannon. "I already put my dollar in."

"I'll give you another dollar," said Colson.

"No," said Shannon again. "It ain't fair."

"Not," said Colson. "It's *not* fair."

Deb tugged her closer. "Please, baby. How about we just get going?"

"No, no, no." Shannon broke free and ran to the other side of the diner. She went into the bathroom and Colson heard the door lock, a metallic slap like a shotgun racking.

"Fuck," said Deb.

She stood and went over to the bathroom. Colson watched as she whispered something through the door and after a moment it opened and Shannon let her in. The door closed again and then locked again. The waitress came for his order and Colson told her not yet. He thought about lighting a cigarette until he remembered the jukebox. He hated to waste music and so he walked over and kicked the machine hard on the side. Customers stared but the jukebox flashed and then it was working. Colson flipped quickly through the playlist, then punched the first of three songs that he thought might just sound good together.

Visual of a Sparrow

FIVE HUNDRED SEVENTY-THREE. Gladys had been so bored once that she'd counted them, every last one of the simple white trailers. Row after row in the dusty pasture. Renaissance Village, FEMA called that hopeless field.

Buses left for the Wal-Mart every couple of hours, and in the beginning Gladys made the trip two or three times a day, something to do. She first met Mrs. Powell at the Wal-Mart; both of them were in the garden section, looking at cat's-eye pansies. They talked about how this was the time of year for pansies—winter—about how much the tiny flowers love the cold, how quick they burn up when summer comes.

Flower talk led to questions about Gladys's circumstances, and her Ninth Ward nightmare earned her a weak cup of sympathy coffee at the snack bar, that and a cash-pay job offer. Mrs. Powell ran a small bed-and-breakfast in the pinewoods, could use someone to help out on the weekends.

The next morning Gladys met her new boss at the entrance to Renaissance Village. She climbed into the old Mercedes and together they rode north to the Brittany House. That had been five months ago.

A pair of domestic peacocks guarded the manicured grounds of the Brittany, and on Friday afternoon their alarm screams announced the arrival of the Atlanta doctor and his fiancée, the only two guests for the weekend. Gladys watched from the shadows as Mrs. Powell greeted them at the door. The doctor's jeweled hands were a flash of gold as he ran them through his silver hair. He paused in the doorway, sizing up the interior of the house like a general approving good ground.

Dr. Cooper was about the same age as Gladys, but the girl— she was at least two decades younger than them both, barely thirty, so far as Gladys could tell. She introduced herself as Megan, then clapped her thin hands together in delight as she stepped in from the February cold. Her skin had a carrot tinge, and stiletto heels peeked out from beneath her tailored jeans. Gladys listened to them click on the pine floor as Mrs. Powell led the couple up the stairs to their room.

Gladys saw Dr. Cooper standing outside on the flagstone patio that overlooked the lake. He raised binoculars to his eyes, began studying a lone blue heron hunting in the distant shallows. Gladys slipped through the French doors. "That's Muggy," she said.

Dr. Cooper looked up from his binoculars and gave a confused grin. "Excuse me?"

"That heron you're looking at," said Gladys. "I call him Muggy because he's cranky with the other birds. He flies off snorting if they crowd him too much."

"Oh." Dr. Cooper laughed. "That's wonderful, Miss Gladys. *Ardea herodias.* Fascinating birds."

Gladys shrugged.

"Did you know that a great blue heron can float on the water just like a goose?"

Gladys rubbed her bare arms for warmth. "Why would I know something like that?"

"I've never seen it myself," Dr. Cooper admitted. "But the books say they can. Even your Muggy." He focused the binoculars on a distant hay field, then handed her the Nikons.

Gladys peered through the lenses. "What am I looking for?"

"See those white birds roosting in that big pine tree?"

"Those are egrets," said Gladys. "We have thousands of egrets."

"Right, *Bubulcus ibis,* very common now—but did you know that cattle egrets have only been in Louisiana for about fifty years?"

Gladys shook her head, and the egrets were sent sliding from left to right in the frame and then back again. "Where'd they come from?"

"Africa," said Dr. Cooper. "Sometime late in the nineteenth century, they say a flock was caught in a storm and blown to South America. At least that's what most bird folks think happened." Gladys continued watching the preening birds; in the low branches, three of them seemed to be fighting. She passed the binoculars back. Dr. Cooper patted her on the arm, a teacher lecturing a child. "And now here they are," he told her. "You see, Miss Gladys. Even the most common birds can be fascinating."

The glass doors opened behind them, and Dr. Cooper turned to greet Megan as she joined them on the patio. Her strawberry blond hair had been washed and blown out, and she wore flared ivory slacks, a wispy chiffon top. Something in Gladys ached to grab hold of that saffron blouse, to feel the strange and feathery crush of the fabric between her callused fingers.

"Oh Lord." Megan rolled her blue eyes and then bumped Dr. Cooper with her small shoulder. "Is Richard boring you with bird talk, Miss Gladys?"

"No, not at all," said Gladys. Then, since her job was to

please all guests, she sly-winked at Megan and added, "It's all very interesting."

Dr. Cooper laughed and draped his blazer around Megan, protecting her from the cold. "I probably am," he said. "Can't be helped, I guess." He returned his binoculars to their patent leather case, then offered Megan his arm like a gentleman in the soaps. "You look beautiful," he told her. "We should get going now if we want to make our reservation."

Gladys followed the couple into the house, then watched from the kitchen as they drove off down the long gravel driveway that led to the highway and town. When they were gone she turned and walked back out onto the patio. In the failing light she tried to remember the first time she ever saw a cattle egret. Growing up in the Delta—working Mississippi fields before her family's big move to the city—there must have been a first time, had to have been. Still, for the life of her Gladys couldn't remember not having those white birds around.

Gladys awoke to the sound of men arguing outside her trailer. She watched through the blinds as Reverend Gray, her neighbor to the right, confronted two boys trying to steal his propane tank. They were young but full grown, ropy teenagers in white tanks and baggy jeans. They slouched through a sermon, then the bigger of the two said something rude. Reverend Gray slapped him hard across the face, and the boys went shuffling off into the night.

It was very dark inside the trailer. Gladys knelt beside her bed and slipped a hand under the mattress. She held her breath until her fingers finally played across the stacked bills, then she glanced at the alarm clock glowing demon red in the corner. In a few hours that clock would be calling for her—telling her to shower, get dressed, go meet Mrs. Powell on the loose-rock shoulder of the highway. She pushed her money farther toward the wall and then lay back down in the small bed, closed her eyes, and fell asleep dreaming of African birds ambushed by a storm, an entire flock sent tumbling across time zones.

Dr. Cooper took his morning coffee at the kitchen table. Gladys sat across from him and listened as he explained that he was hoping to see a Henslow's sparrow over the weekend, a dwindling species that wintered in what was left of the country's longleaf-pine savannas.

Gladys nodded and then brushed butter atop the last of her scratch biscuits. Dr. Cooper had a satellite map spread out across the lacquered-cypress table, and the space photo showed the refuge that bordered Mrs. Powell's property. He told her that he planned to scout while Megan slept in, and so Gladys foil-wrapped three biscuits for him to take along in his daypack. She wished him luck in finding his rare bird as he walked out into the still-dark morning. He was wearing a tan jacket that had at least a dozen pockets. Gladys knew nothing of a Henslow's, had never seen such a creature so far as she knew.

By the second day after the storm, summer had settled back in. The sun beat down on the city and made tar-black shingles hot enough to blister skin. Gladys stood atop the roof of her sunk and crumbling home and watched a stream of debris float by: a doll's head, some tires, a styrofoam cooler that she fished in with a stick. A forty-ounce bottle of Country Club lay inside the dry cooler. Gladys knew better but she was also very thirsty. She unscrewed the cap and began to drink.

The beer was warm and stale and left Baptist Gladys spinning in the sun so that later, when the game warden saved her, she stumbled getting into his boat and fell hard against the others—friends and neighbors who caught her and told her that she would be okay now. As they picked their way back through the Lower Nine, the whine of the outboard set hungry dogs to barking. People hollered from here and there but the boat, already full, kept on.

Somewhere along St. Claude they surprised a flock of wild ducks and sent them splashing for the sky. The game warden told Gladys that they were teal—greenwings—and she watched as they took flight. They circled her neighborhood once, twice, then left altogether to put down in some other distant corner of the flooded city.

Megan appeared in the kitchen not long after Dr. Cooper had left. The peacocks crowed from their roost in the live oak, and Megan laughed as she told Gladys how much she loved the morning cry of peacocks. How they reminded her of a wonderful week she and Richard had spent on a spice plantation, guests of his partner's family in some far-off place called Kerala.

Her tinted hair was secured atop her head with a red plastic clip, and she wore satin warm-ups the color of Christmas tinsel. Gladys watched as the girl wet her lips with orange juice, then nibbled at the corner of a cathead biscuit. She was fascinated by this Megan. What could she be thinking about at that moment? What had her life been like as a child? When she made love to her doctor, was she a wild little thing?

Megan returned to her room to shower at about the same time that Gladys heard the redbirds—the first birds—begin to sing in the twilight before dawn.

For months Mrs. Powell had tried to bait Gladys, leaving fives, then tens, lying loose around the house. But Gladys knew better and had always resisted—she left the money folded neatly on the nearest table every damned time. Finally Mrs. Powell came to treat her with something like trust and would leave Gladys in charge so that she could meet her friends for bridge at the club in Baton Rouge. Gladys figured those card-club Saturdays, in command of that beautiful house, were the closest she would ever come to living like the princess her father had always insisted that she was.

With her two guests fed and the kitchen cleaned, Gladys was now free until lunch. It was time for her morning walk. She changed from her housedress into blue jeans, then put on old tennis shoes and a heavy corduroy coat. Her canvas bag was in the hall closet. She filled a thermos with coffee and struck out.

The nature trail led from behind the Brittany into the refuge, meandering through a soft forest of magnolia and willow before the woods opened up onto a vast savanna dotted with fire-scarred pines. Day was breaking, and a thin line of brilliant orange spread across the eastern horizon. Gladys watched as the sunrise was swallowed up by the aluminum sky—damp and cold and threatening rain—and was reminded of her long-dead blacksmith grandfather. Of the moment when he would drop iron, hammered even and glowing, into gray water to cool and to strengthen.

At the edge of the savanna, beavers had dammed several streams that drained into the forest, and a small pond had formed. Gladys spread a worn blanket out over a patch of sandy soil hidden within a wax-myrtle thicket. Two beavers were still awake and working. Gladys sat and watched them dive alongside the dam, desperate to finish repairing some invisible breach.

She was on her second mug of coffee when she spotted Megan walking along the south fork of the trail. The path ran beneath Gladys, then ended at a washout bank of the pond. Megan approached, and the beavers vanished beneath the surface before the girl ever even knew that they existed.

Megan settled onto the trunk of a fallen tupelo, just a few feet from the bank, then started tracing sand circles with the toe of her hiking boot. Gladys crouched lower in the thicket. She had developed a servant's sense of when people wanted their privacy and knew better than to disturb the girl. Besides, Gladys enjoyed studying her. The way she tossed pebbles into the beaver pond. The way she removed a colorful handkerchief from her ski jacket and unwrapped a cigarette lighter, a single secret joint. The way she could almost feel her worrying about Dr. Cooper as distant storm clouds commenced their slow roll across the savanna. The way she laughed out loud when the rain began to fall and sent her jogging back up the trail toward the house.

Walking home, shivering beneath her raincoat, Gladys could still smell the linger of marijuana but noticed that—in a few low spots on the muddy trail, interspersed with the tracks of deer and feral hogs—Megan's small footprints were already beginning to fill with water.

"I found a field alive with Henslow's," said Dr. Cooper. He was sipping chamomile tea by the fireplace with Megan curled at his feet. She leaned against his leg, cupping her own mug with both hands as she listened to him. "They chirp, almost like an insect. I heard them all around me before the storm came."

Gladys was polishing a hammered-copper vase that Mrs. Powell had purchased in Mexico. "How many did you see?" she asked.

Dr. Cooper laughed. "Not a single visual, Miss Gladys. They stuck to the ground cover, and I couldn't flush the first one."

"The rain should let up in a few hours." Gladys returned the vase to its place on the mantel. Dr. Cooper's jacket of pockets hung dripping from a hook beneath it. "Maybe you could try again this afternoon."

"Yes," said Dr. Cooper. "We were discussing that very idea while you were making our tea." His fingers danced across his fiancée's head. "Megan has even agreed to help me work the field. That'll double my chances of kicking one up."

Megan smiled and leaned back as Dr. Cooper began stroking her hair. Her eyes were closed and she spoke without opening them. "Would you like to join us, Miss Gladys?"

"Excuse me?"

"Would you like to come along?" Megan rolled her head along the contour of Dr. Cooper's knee, then finally focused on Gladys. Last night the girl's eyes had been blue; today they were hazel. "It might be your only chance to ever see one," she said.

"Absolutely," said Dr. Cooper. "Please come along. I need all the troops I can muster."

Gladys watched the firelight play off the antique wine bottles embedded in the chimney. The day before her sister had called with another invitation to join them in their Houston apartment. More thrown-together charity for the never-married Gladys. "Storm or no storm," Loretta had said, "Daddy didn't get us out the fields to have you become some old bitch's slave."

"If you really don't mind," Gladys told her guests. "I do think I'd like to tag along."

The field was just as Dr. Cooper had promised: alive with the cricket calls of sparrows. He spaced Gladys and Megan off on either side of him, and they moved as a line toward the bank of a narrow creek that ran through the flatwoods.

They were armed with snapped boughs of pine, and Dr. Cooper ordered them to make noise as they lashed their way across the field of khaki winter-dried grass. He laughed and said they reminded him of low-caste beaters on a tiger hunt. Megan grinned and challenged the sparrows to show themselves, then Dr. Cooper slapped at her flat ass with his pine branch. The two of them soon fell into a conversation about the waitress from the night before, how right she had been about the trout amandine.

Gladys had nothing to say. She tried calling for the sparrows to appear but felt silly and quieted.

"Come on now," said Dr. Cooper. "Help us out, Miss Gladys."

Since he was, after all, a guest of the Brittany, Gladys began to hum and then sing the only verses she could remember from one of her father's songs, a song that he would sing in the picking fields.

> What good is sunshine when you are blue?
> When there is no one who cares for you?
> The birds are singing songs by the score,
> You just wonder who they're singing for.
> I've got the blues,
> But I'm just too damn mean to cry.

Gladys reached the last verse, then turned and realized that she had pushed far ahead of the line. Dr. Cooper and Megan had paused and were listening to her sing. Gladys stared back at them; she was embarrassed and wanted to go home now.

"Don't stop," said Dr. Cooper. "In fact, we're not moving another step until you've taught us both that song."

"Yes," said Megan. "Please."

Before Gladys could refuse, the line collapsed in on itself and they huddled around her. Vapor trails of steam escaped from their three mouths to mingle and then disappear. Gladys whispered the verses of the old blues song a couple of times before they spread back out and began to sing, an off-key wall of music pushing across the field—and, Gladys supposed, forcing invisible sparrows against the creek bank.

They walked on and Gladys spotted some movement in the grass a few feet to her left. A small chestnut bird ran like a mouse through the brush, then buried itself in a clump of broken broom sedge. Gladys waved to Dr. Cooper, motioning for him to come quietly. He reached her side and Gladys knelt down. She pointed to a spray of delicate tail feathers, the only part of the sparrow that remained visible, exposed.

Megan had joined them as well. "Is it a Henslow's?" she whispered.

"*Ammodramus henslowii*," said Dr. Cooper, and at the sound of its name the sparrow bolted, took off running down another tunnel of brush. "Make it fly, goddamn it! Make it fly!" Dr. Cooper shoved Megan and then Gladys in the back, and as they stumbled forward the sparrow finally flushed. It flew low and quick across the muddy creek, then lit down on the lip of a pitcher plant.

Gladys had fallen hard onto her knees. She heard Megan begin whimpering beside her, but concentrated on watching the Henslow's. The tiny creature seemed to be watching her right back and considering her, regarding her. Dr. Cooper ordered Gladys to be still, but when he spoke the perched sparrow chirped and dropped back to earth.

There came a second chirp, and then it was swallowed up by the underbrush once again.

Burke's Maria

*A*N OUTPOST CAMP *moves through virgin timber, pushing panthers and ivory-bills deeper into the swamp. Working with their own tools, paid by the kill, hard men drop an enormous cypress in the direction of a fresh canal. They sound the steam whistle and collect at the company pull boat.*

A thick cable is stretched a half-mile back into the swamp, to the dead tree. A holler down the line and the drum begins to turn, drawing the log to pull boat; the men, smoking and laughing, ride her like a sled.

The cypress is bound to others floating in the canal, a great raft to be led out the swamp to the Pass Manchac tracks, loaded onto an Illinois Central flatcar, and hauled south to New Orleans.

She breaks free in a storm and wanders for weeks through the bayous and canals until one cold, quiet night she has absorbed enough water and sinks, nestling like a lost ship in the silt bottom of a forgotten spur.

Choupique season opened in December and ran three months through the winter spawn. On the final week Burke fished the back, dead-end waters above North Pass, stretching small nets along the trenasses and washout gaps where bayous bled into the swamp. Here, the big females, roe heavy, would follow the high water over breeched bayou banks, then deposit their eggs in shallow nests that had been tail-scraped in the soft mud by stud males, ready and waiting for a home to guard.

He set close to thirty nets Monday evening and dawn the next morning pulled in fifty-odd females—ugly prehistoric creatures looking more reptile than fish. Only a few of the fishermen around Manchac bothered messing with choupique, chasing caviar. Most stuck to the Pontchartrain, fishing the blue crabs that paid the bills until spring shrimp.

Burke was different. He'd take deck-hand work on a shrimper, maybe help a friend move crab traps around the lake, but for the most part he stuck to the old ways, the freshwater. Men teased him for that, called him a swamp rat. No matter. To Burke, the big lake held nothing but fool's gold. Hang your hat on crabs, shrimp—you're always just a hurricane, a seized motor, away from losing everything. And so he diversified, threw a wide, steady net across life.

Burke made a dusty circle in the clamshell parking lot of Sullivan's, then backed his boat trailer up to the loading dock. One of the Mexicans gave a *whoa* whistle, and Burke slid out of his pickup. It was a perfect day, blue-skied and beautiful. He saw Avery standing by the scales while they weighed out his crabs. Burke waved, and his skinny cousin shuffled over. He was dressed the same as Burke: blue jeans and white shrimp boots, a thick flannel shirt. His long brown hair was pinned back with an orange bandanna.

"So how go the mudfish, old man?"

Burke smiled and climbed up into his skiff, a plain white Reno. "That's it for the season."

"Make any money?"

"Did all right." Burke began pulling choupique from the

live well and passing them down to the Mexicans. "How's crab-
bing?"

"Same old." Avery lit a new cigarette off the cherry of his
last. "Puts beer on the table."

"I found a great big cypress last week."

"Yeah?"

"Yeah, sunk back in a canal off Middle Bayou."

"Think Lonnie will let us borrow the barge?"

"Already talked to him." Burke lifted his mesh Saints cap
with his left hand, then rubbed at a sideburn with his right.
"Free Friday?"

"Hell, Cousin. I'm always free."

Burke nodded as the Mexicans stacked the last of his
choupique into a wheelbarrow and rolled them into the proc-
essing plant.

Almost an entire wall of Sam Sullivan's office was a window,
the back side of a two-way mirror that looked out over the floor
of the plant. Rows of Mexican women worked the refrigerated
room, handpicking long piles of steaming crabs.

Sam was old and kind, a good and decent man. He handed
Burke a Coke, and they watched the foreman pull five women
off the line. The Mexicans wore hairnets and paper masks, long
white coats over layers of cheap sweatpants and sweatshirts
that Sam bought in bulk from the Wal-Mart in Hammond.
Burke thought one of the women might be Maria but couldn't
be sure.

Sam went to his desk and they settled into chairs. "You had
a good season."

"I guess."

"So what's next?"

"Thought I'd rest up a few days, then start pulling cypress."

Sam nodded, his attention on the floor of the plant. The foreman led the Mexicans to a stainless steel table and began laying out Burke's catch. With sharp knives, two women opened the bellies of still-breathing choupique, passing great blue-black sacs of caviar to the others to wash, clean, and weigh. They finished and the foreman scratched down a number on a scrap of paper that he pressed against Sam's trick window.

"That fair enough, Burke?"

"Sure, fair enough."

But Burke wasn't paying attention; he was watching the doe-eyed girl who had tugged her mask down beneath her chin. He'd like to think this was a hello for him but knew that, from her side of things, Maria could see nothing but her own reflection. Her young, pretty face floating in the glass.

The Mexicans lived in a cinder-block bunkhouse behind Sullivan's. Most of the men—the husbands, brothers, and fathers—they were all gone, had left after the storm to find work in the city. There was good money to be made in New Orleans, cash for roofing houses, pulling rotten sheetrock.

Burke's small red-brick home was just across the railroad tracks from the Mexicans' bunkhouse. That evening he was storing the last of his nets when Maria appeared, stepping out of the right-of-way and into his yard. She was quiet but knew more English than she liked to let on. Burke thought that in her snow-white sweats she looked damned close to an angel.

Maria crossed Burke's yard and he followed her into his house. He stayed clear while she washed his filthy clothes, vacuumed and mopped the floors. She finished and he went to his bedroom closet, gathered a handful of the caviar cash from the hidden cigar box—the place where he kept those cash earnings that the government would never know of.

In the laundry room Burke passed Maria her weekly twenty. He then offered dinner and an extra hundred, asked that she stay awhile. As always, Maria accepted with a smile.

After Burke had showered he pulled back the slick curtain and there she was, waiting with a warm, clean towel she had taken from the dryer. She was wearing one of his T-shirts now—a cheap white V-neck. Burke stepped to her, and she raised her arms just like a little girl. He slid the thin shirt up and over her head.

A small cross hung from a chain around Maria's neck. Burke tried to kiss her and she placed the crucifix in her mouth. She bit down on the silver and he wrapped the towel around them both. Maria hugged his wet body and then they began a slow shuffle-dance out of the bathroom.

"You do not trust me, Señor Burke?" Maria sat on the edge of the bed as he searched the nightstand for a condom.

"Burke, just Burke."

"Burke."

"Of course I trust you," he said, slipping into a Trojan. "It's just something everyone does in America."

"Then you no good Catholic."

Burke lay back on the bed, and Maria climbed on top and took him inside. The silver cross was swinging in the space between them, back and forth, back and forth, a hypnotist's pendulum. "No," he said, his voice rough. "I don't guess I'm much of one at all."

Maria frowned and ran her fingers over the scars on his chest, groaning as she moved over him. Her black hair tickled his face and she rose up and off him when he shuddered, went soft. Burke flipped her over and used his hand on her until she came, or at least pretended to, then left her tangled in the bed sheets while he searched for their supper.

He made fresh rice that they shared in the kitchen, ate with the last of yesterday's courtbouillon. Later, Maria brought their coffee out onto the porch, and she was singing a quiet song when one of the older women crossed the tracks and came calling. The señora scolded Maria in Spanish, then led her home like some stray village goat.

It was marketed and sold as Cajun caviar, the roe cut from choupique. Burke dreamed about taking Maria down to the city some night, over to one of the restaurants in the Quarter. They would find a fine place with ivory tablecloths, order champagne and a dozen raw oysters topped with beads of caviar, his caviar. He would show her that a choupique wasn't just some trash fish, that he wasn't just some dirty fisherman—that, in the end, they both contributed to something classy, something appreciated, something delicious.

A little before midnight the phone rang, a call from the bartender at the up-the-road cut-and-shoot. Miss Cindy coughed hard and told Burke that the place was empty save for Avery and the Daigle brothers, glaring at one another from across the room. She figured there would be trouble soon, trouble no doubt.

Burke sighed and then eased out of bed, into his jeans and the undershirt that still smelled of Maria. The sliver moon was a day off new, the air brisk but not too cold. He drove to the Lastchance, coming through the door just in time to see Duke Daigle push Avery down. Miss Cindy screeched a take-it-outside and both Daigles fell back at the sight of Burke. Avery was writhing on the plywood floor, a toppled turtle struggling to right itself. Burke shook hands with Duke, and Avery went still, appeared to fall asleep.

Duke pulled his wristwatch out the front pocket of his jeans and put it back on. "Man, Burke, we was just in here playing pool when he started saying that we was running his traps." He pointed at his brother, now slumped against the silent jukebox. "He punched Peanut in back the head."

"Well?"

"It's true," hollered Peanut.

"No," said Burke. "The traps, I mean."

Duke shook his head. "Our skiff's been on the bank for a week. Bent prop, ask anybody."

Burke went to the bar and bought beers for the Daigles. "Y'all do me a favor and take him home, try and keep from leaving him in a ditch."

Peanut pressed the cold can of Bud Light to the back of his head and winced. "Sure thing," he said. He helped his brother peel Avery off the floor, and they dragged him outside like a wounded soldier.

Burke watched them leave and then took a seat at the bar. Miss Cindy was studying him from behind a cloud of smoke. "Bachelor Burke," she said.

"Miss Cindy."

"Want something?"

Burke thought on it. "A little SoCo on a lot of ice," he said finally.

Miss Cindy fixed his drink and then flashed her yellow teeth. "You know, people been talking, saying you must have the cleanest house in Manchac."

Burke sipped his Southern Comfort. "That's not really saying much," he said.

"Well, they also saying you're gonna get trapped with a Mexican baby."

"That right?"

"That's what they saying." She smiled and winked at him. "You think you're her only customer?"

"I mind my own business."

"Your mama would have wanted me to say something."

Burke ran his finger through a puddle that had formed on the bar. "People always gonna talk, Miss Cindy. That's what they do."

Sam Sullivan paid Burke to night-watch his buster crabs, and twice—first at midnight, then again at four A.M.—Burke would cross the railroad tracks and unlock the shed, pull molted crabs from the water before their tender new shells went to leather.

He checked the tanks on his way home from the Last-chance, stored seven dripping softshells in the refrigerator, and then waited for an eighth to finish shucking. Cold winter rain began to fall, pinging the tin roof of the shed. Next door, the Mexicans slept in their bunkhouse. Burke thought of Maria and imagined that she might be awake at that late hour—imagined that maybe, just maybe, she might be alone and thinking of him.

Rain fell steady for the next two days. Fishermen left their traps soaking in the lake, and Burke lazed on the couch, watching satellite during the cloud breaks. Come Thursday morning the Mexicans had no more crabs to pick. The few men who had not left for New Orleans killed time playing cards on the loading dock, while the women did laundry in the washer/dryer on the back porch of the bunkhouse.

Maria was waiting her turn for the Kenmore when Burke stepped outside and hollered, Come on. She turned and he waved, then he jogged over to help carry her laundry bags across the tracks.

She mixed his clothes from yesterday in with her own, had them spinning clean when the señora came for her again. She marched right up Burke's porch and banged on his door. He answered and the woman pushed past him, grabbed Maria by the hair. Burke stepped between them and Maria shook free, then let fly a string of border-town curses that chased the señora back to the bunkhouse.

An hour later the next person to visit was Sam, sent by the Mexicans on account of the situation. Burke met him at the door with Maria by his side.

"I'm in a bind," said Sam.

"How's that?"

"The women won't work with her no more, Burke. I've got to get rid of her." Sam cleared his throat. "They done threw all her things outside already. The best I can do is take her up to catch a Greyhound. I'll buy her a bus ticket to wherever she wants."

Burke saw the Mexicans gathered and watching from across the tracks. He shook his head. "Do me a favor and go fetch her stuff," he said. "I'll take her to Ponchatoula if it comes to that."

"You sure?"

"It's my mess."

Sam grunted and left.

Burke turned to Maria. *"Gracias,"* she said to him. "Thank you." He nodded and then held her. She began to cry and they stayed that way for a long time, all the way up until Sam returned carrying a garbage bag filled with her few rain-soaked possessions.

That night, Burke passed on the condom. Maria noticed and kissed him for the first time. Their teeth clicked together as they moved across the bed. She laughed and brought her lips to his ear, breathed Spanish whispers until he was done, spent.

His wallet was on the nightstand and Burke went for it now. He fished out some twenties that Maria refused. "No more money." She waved her hand across the room. "All of this is enough." She closed her eyes, and Burke wondered just what all of this was.

He would sometimes watch this television show about commercial fishermen, crabbers up on the Bering Sea. He watched an episode while Maria slept, her warm legs locked around his own. The captain was worried about some pots being covered by the approaching ice pack, expensive gear carelessly lost.

What the captain didn't mention was how a lost trap becomes a ghost trap and keeps fishing, keeps killing. How his bait would bring crabs until it was gone. How the caught crabs would then begin to starve, become bait themselves as others entered to attack the dead and dying.

In time the captain's stray pots would be packed full of dead crabs, then add more still whenever enough broken shells crumbled away and made room. Just putting some dollar amount on the cost of lost gear ignored all that. To Burke, money didn't come close to covering the damage that captain was doing to the world.

Avery breezed into Burke's house Friday morning, saying hi to Maria as if he'd expected her to be there. She nodded at him from the living room sofa, and the cousins stepped outside to talk.

"Take it you got home all right the other night," said Burke.

Avery laughed. "Yeah, sure," he said. "Thanks for the help."

"No problem." Burke slid his hand up the sleeve of his T-shirt, rubbed the spot on his shoulder where Maria had bitten him. "You ready?"

"I'm ready."

Burke nodded toward the house. "Mind if she comes along?"

Avery grinned and shook his head.

They launched Burke's skiff in the canal that ran under the interstate, then tied onto the winch barge docked behind Lonnie Carson's house. It was cold out on the water, and Maria huddled close as Burke steered the skiff. His tan duck jacket was wrapped tight around her narrow shoulders. He was uncomfortable now in just his T-shirt but was careful not to let on.

Burke towed the winch barge up North Pass into Middle Bayou, then down a little spur canal. He pointed at Avery, and Maria laughed. His cousin had stripped down to his underwear and was laid out on the bow, shivering as he tried to squeeze into a secondhand wetsuit.

With the high water they were able to pull the barge far into the swamp. Near the end of the spur Burke shut down the outboard, then began searching with a push pole until he connected with the sinker—the ancient timber resting like buried treasure at the bottom of the canal.

The cousins positioned the barge above the sinker, and Avery slipped over the side of the skiff, into the dark water. Burke handed him slack cable from the winch, and Avery took a deep breath. He disappeared beneath the surface.

A half a dozen shallow dives and Avery was able to work the thick cable through the mud and then back around the circumference of the log. Burke started up the diesel winch and took in the slack, motioning for Maria to stay clear as the cable went tight. The winch began to whine under the strain.

No give. Avery swore and Burke killed the winch. Again Avery dove, scraping more silt out from under the trapped cypress with a steel trowel. Another six dives and he surfaced, gasping. His face was pink and marbled. With a thumbs-up he gave Burke the go-ahead to spin the winch.

A second time Burke asked Maria to step aside, only now she refused and came to him, reaching out with her hands so that one rested atop his head, the other on the winch. She smiled as she spoke hushed words that Burke took to be a prayer, maybe a blessing. She pulled away and he shrugged. Burke flipped the switch and laughed as bubbles came and he felt it, as they all felt it, the swamp beginning to give up the great cypress, lost for some hundred years.

For the better part of the day they worked freeing the cypress, and once the log was secured to the barge they made the slow tow back to Manchac. At the interstate canal they turned off the pass and pushed on to Lonnie's. In the distance they could see the old man weed-eating between the Roman columns of sinkers that lay drying on his lawn, waiting their turn for the sawmill.

The day had warmed, and Lonnie wore loose overalls but no shirt as he worked. He clapped his hands hot damn when he saw their catch, then jogged into his barn and brought out the tractor. Maria went to shore and watched the cousins fasten the thick tow chains. They released the sinker from the barge and gave Lonnie a go wave.

The glistening black timber slid dripping from the canal. Lonnie pulled the log up onto the bank, positioning it with the others before crawling down from his tractor. He was making his measurements when Burke brought Maria over and showed her the base—the spot where the crosscut saw of a long-dead man had taken the tree, virgin cypress like the world hadn't seen in three generations.

Maria's hand went to the trunk, the saw scar. She moved her fingers across the thin bands of rings, and Burke saw that she understood because she was counting softly, counting out the years. She counted *uno, dos, tres* before her big brown eyes grew even bigger and she realized that she had a thousand more years to go.

Lonnie haggled with them over the price before he finally took his cut for the winch barge and offered a big number that Burke split sixty-forty with Avery. The cousins straddled the sinker as they counted out the cash. Satisfied, they untied the skiff from the barge and idled back to the launch.

Driving home, they stopped at the little concrete market between the highway and the boat works. Burke was icing down a case of beer when the Daigle brothers pulled up, back in business and on their way to Sullivan's to sell their catch. Maria sipped grape soda while the men talked along the edge of the blacktop. The cousins swapped six beers for a half hamper of fat crabs that they took back to Burke's to boil.

Maria went into the house while they set up the burner in Burke's driveway. Avery began heating water and Burke checked on her, found her already asleep. He watched Maria for a moment—this beautiful young woman asleep in his bed—then went to the closet and dug the cigar box out from the back corner. He added Lonnie's cash to his choupique money, the little he made off tending the softshells.

"The crabs are ready?"

Burke jumped at the sound of her voice, banging his head against the side of the closet.

Maria laughed. "I scared you?"

"No, no." Burke closed the closet door and sat down on the corner of the bed. "Thought you were sleeping, that's all."

They moved a picnic table to the driveway and spread the boiled crabs out across layers of newspaper. In the warm sun it felt almost like spring. Avery rolled down the windows of

Burke's pickup, and they listened to old country music and ate crabs, drank their cold beer.

Maria sat opposite the cousins. A foot teased her bare calf and she teased back, smiling at Burke until she realized that Avery had come courting. She withdrew and shook her head, let him know that their thing was done, over.

Avery glared back at her as he ripped loose a claw. He smashed the shell open with the bottom of an empty beer bottle and Maria flinched, then returned to cleaning her own crabs. She was focused, serious, her hands a blur as she sorted the meat into neat piles of lump, backfin, claw.

Burke laughed and Maria looked up, blushing when she saw that he had been watching her work. Then, more laughter, laughter from across the tracks. The señora, her tormentor, was cackling like a goblin as she waved a mask and a hairnet.

Maria's eyes watered and she excused herself. Her sweet crabmeat cooled on Burke's table while, back inside his house, she watched Mexican soap operas on the satellite she'd already taught herself to work.

Burke awoke and the bedroom was twilight gray. He turned and saw that the alarm clock had been unplugged. He had slept through the night, missed both checks on Sullivan's buster crabs.

And Maria was gone—her side of the bed cool, cold even. Burke sat up and shook his beer-thick head. He looked around the room and understood all at once that she had packed up and left, disappeared sometime during the night. He hurried to the closet and then dropped to his knees, sliding his hand under spare blankets until his fingers met the cigar box.

Burke opened the lid and relaxed when he saw his money —the neat stacks of crisp bills all there—Mother of Christ, thank God. He dressed quickly, then went into the den and woke Avery, asleep on the couch.

"What is it?" Avery rubbed an eye with the meat of his palm.

"Maria's gone."

Avery swung his bare feet to the floor and sat looking at him. "I heard somebody leave out the door around midnight," he said. "Figured it was you checking the crabs."

Burke kicked Avery's jeans closer to the couch. "Come on," he said.

"She's long gone, you know that."

"Maybe."

"Ain't no maybe about it."

"You gonna help me find her or not?"

"Yeah, Christ. Just give me five minutes, okay?"

Burke went outside and started the pickup. The air was chill again. The engine began its slow idle to warm as he crossed the tracks and slipped inside the slumbering bunkhouse. No sign of Maria. A sharp whistle and he heard a train rumble by, separating him from his truck. Cut off and restless, his search delayed, Burke left the bunkhouse and went to check on the busters. He stared at them and sighed, hoped Sam wouldn't notice just how many of those softshells he'd let go to leather.

South of Hammond the lime green longleafs give way to cypress as the interstate enters the once-great swamp that flanks Lake Pontchartrain. A truck driver hears a rattle and pulls off at Manchac, parking on the shoulder of the ramp while he checks the thick chains binding his load of creosote-soaked Mississippi pine.

He is stepping back up into his rig when a young woman approaches carrying a garbage bag. She is wearing jeans and a jacket. Her T-shirt is too big for her, and it meets in a plunging V at a point just between her small breasts. A silver cross winks in the head-

lights, and the girl shivers as she begs a ride in shy, shaky English. The driver smiles and says, Of course, señorita. I'm headed south to the city, let me know just how far you want to go.

In New Orleans the interstate cuts through City Park. The sun is up and the girl can see the migrants camped along the bayou, the old tents, the blue tarps taken from roof jobs. This, she thinks, is the place. She asks out and the trucker eases onto the shoulder, reaching for her as she opens the door. His big and damp hand finds her wrist but the girl is able to twist loose. She slides free of the cab and he curses her. The massive rig rolls forward and she tumbles to the asphalt, tears her jeans.

The girl sits on the side of the interstate, whimpering as she pulls bits of rock from a burnt knee. She hears a whistle and looks up. Men are watching her from behind the chainlink fence that borders the park. They call to her in Spanish. She stands and limps across the interstate. She goes to the men. She throws them her bag. She is searching for her father's face even as she begins to climb, to rise.

Acknowledgments

First: Sylvia, all my love and gratitude for being the absolute best thing ever to happen to me. Without you, I don't write; hell, I'm not so sure I even smile.

Thanks to all the wonderful and generous people at the Stanford University Creative Writing Department, the Bread Loaf Writers' Conference, and Houghton Mifflin Harcourt—as well as the incredibly supportive and understanding folks at Watson, Blanche, Wilson and Posner in Baton Rouge.

Thanks also to Liz Lee, Nicole Angeloro, Lisa Glover, Tracy Roe, Michael Collier, Tom Jenks, Bret Lott, Pia Z. Ehrhardt, and, of course, the amazing Antonya Nelson.

I owe so much to the fantastic writing teachers I've had along the way: Brother Ray Bulliard, Mary Jane Ryals, Amanda Boyden, John L'Heureux, Elizabeth Tallent, Colm Tóibín, Tobias Wolff, and the late Brother Bill Parsons. Thank you all.

My deepest appreciation to the following journals and magazines where previous versions of several stories have appeared: *Sea Oats Review, ByLine,* the *Southeast Review, New Delta Review, Louisiana Literature, Southern Gothic, StoryQuarterly,* the *Southern Review, Epoch,* and *Narrative.*

I made a promise to my older brother a long, long time ago—and so this book goes to him (thanks, Matt, I'll love and miss you forever). Still, Mom and Dad, please know that you're my twin heroes, and I love you both much more than I could ever express.

Finally, thank you to my family and friends. Many of you I haven't seen in quite some time, but you're all under my skin and with me (in a good way). You've given me so much to write about over the years—so thank you, thank you, thank you.

Bread Loaf and the Bakeless Prizes

The Katharine Bakeless Nason Literary Publication Prizes were established in 1995 to expand the Bread Loaf Writers' Conference's commitment to the support of emerging writers. Endowed by the LZ Francis Foundation, the prizes commemorate Middlebury College patron Katharine Bakeless Nason and launch the publication careers of a poet, a fiction writer, and a creative nonfiction writer annually. Winning manuscripts are chosen in an open national competition by a distinguished judge in each genre. Winners are published by Houghton Mifflin Harcourt Publishing Company in Mariner paperback original.

2008 JUDGES

Antonya Nelson, *fiction*

Tom Bissell, *nonfiction*

Eavan Boland, *poetry*